BOOTS & WINGS

UGLY STICK SALOON SERIES BOOK #15

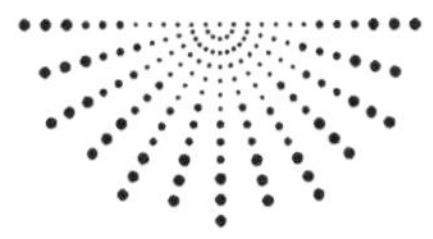

MYLA JACKSON

TWISTED PAGE INC

BOOTS & WINGS

UGLY STICK SALOON SERIES BOOK #15

New York Times & USA Today
Bestselling Author

ELLE JAMES

writing as

MYLA JACKSON

Ebook ISBN: 978-1-62695-029-0

Print ISBN: 978-1-62695-046-7

This book is dedicated to everyone who has had to make difficult choices. Some are easier than others. The world, and life, are full of possibilities. Embrace them!

AUTHOR'S NOTE

Enjoy other Ugly Stick Saloon books by Myla Jackson
Boots & Chaps (#1)
Boots & Sex Ed (#2)
Boots & Leather (#3)
Boots & Promises (#4)
Boots & Bareback (#5)
Boots & Dirty Tricks (#6)
Boots & Lace (#7)
Boots & Roses (#8)
Boots & Buckles (#9)
Boots & the Wishes (#10)
Boots & Twisters (#11)
Boots & the Bachelor (#12)
Boots & The Rogue (#13)
Boots & The Heartbreaker (#14)
Boots & Wings (#15)

Visit Mylajackson.com for more information
Visit her alter ego Elle James at ellejames.com
Join Elle James and Myla Jackson's Newsletter at
http://ellejames.com/ElleContact.htm

CHAPTER ONE

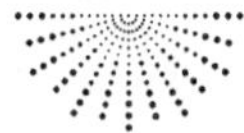

"*D*id you lock and secure the plane and helicopter?" Tucker Maddox asked from behind his sturdy metal desk.

His brother, Jake, carried his flight bag through the door. The heat and dust of the Texas summer followed him inside. "Done. Buttoned up, secure and fueled up for tomorrow."

"Good." Tucker closed his logbook. "Maybe we'll get out of here early today."

Jake stretched his arms over his head. "We deserve a little rest and relaxation after two weeks of non-stop gigs. Oh, and my last client tipped me a hundred dollars. The beer's on me at the Ugly Stick Saloon tonight."

Tucker cocked his brows. "You have a five a.m. flight in the morning. Should you be drinking tonight?"

Jake shook his head. "What's one beer gonna hurt? After the month we've had, we deserve a little fun."

"It's only been really bad the past two weeks."

"My point exactly." Jake shoved his flight gear onto the shelf behind the customer counter. "Besides, I think it's ladies night. By the time we get *cleaned* up, they'll be *liquored* up and ready for some Maddox lovin'."

"Can't you wait for that beer until we go to Nick's bachelor party? Audrey promised a hot stripper for the event and she's closing the saloon for us after eleven. Should be a good time."

"That's next weekend. I want a beer and good company now." Jake dropped into his chair, kicked up his heels, plunked them onto his desk and leaned back with his hands behind his neck. "I can't believe Nick's taking the plunge. Do you suppose it's because he's over thirty and starting to feel his age?"

"Hey." Tucker frowned. "I'm over thirty, and you'll be thirty in four months."

Jake closed his eyes and stretched again. "Don't tell me you've been thinking about settling down and raising a family."

Over the past month, working as much as he had, Tucker had been thinking just that. He wasn't getting any younger, and he didn't want to be alone all his life. When he'd left the army four years ago, he'd put relationships on hold until he got his affairs in order.

He and Jake started the business, almost going bankrupt in the first year.

Thankfully the business kept Tucker from dwelling on his past. Coming off active duty, he'd been plagued by nightmares of his days and nights as a Black Hawk helicopter pilot. Over time, the dreams had dissipated. He'd weaned himself off sleep aids a year ago and hadn't taken them since. Lately, instead of dreaming about RPG attacks and evacuating wounded warriors, a feisty female haunted his dreams, making him wake up in the middle of the night. Not yelling, thrashing and reliving a nightmare, but aroused, hard and ready for lovemaking.

Going home to the small ranch he and his brother had inherited from their parents was okay, but it would be a whole lot better with a woman to warm his bed. And not just any woman. Molly O'Brien.

The youngest of the O'Brien clan, Molly had been a pigtailed pest tagging along behind her brothers when Tucker was in high school. But the girl had since grown up. The beautiful spitfire hit every one of the requirements on his list.

Smart, beautiful, loved kids and she had a heart as big as the state of Texas.

"I have to admit, with Nick's bachelor party coming up, it got me thinking along those lines as well," Jake said.

Tucker snorted. "Like you could settle for one

female when there is...what do you call it...oh yes, a smorgasbord of women to choose from."

Jake shrugged. "In case you haven't noticed, the pickin's are getting slimmer the older we get. Nick's marrying Lacey. Audrey and Jackson Gray Wolf hooked up and are expecting their first kid. Libby's with Jackson's brothers, Mark and Luke. Connor Mason snagged Kendall, and rodeo champion, Grant Raleigh, took Mona off the market—"

Tucker raised his hand. "Okay, okay. I get it. We're running out of options. But that doesn't mean we have to hurry out and propose to the first unattached female we find."

"No, but if we don't move quickly on the ones we like, we may get beat out by someone else."

Tucker crossed his arms and stared across the desk at his younger brother. "So, what are you going to do about it?"

Jake raked a hand through his thick, black hair, making it stand on end. "I never thought I'd say this, but I think it's time I got hitched."

"Just like that?"

His brother shrugged. "I'm not getting any younger."

"You're twenty-nine, not an old man. Got someone in mind?" Tucker waited for his answer. Jake had been out with nearly every woman in the tri-county area. For him to settle on one was a big deal.

"I don't know. I've only been out with one lady more than once. She's sassy, sexy and independent enough she could put up with the type of work we're in. She loves the outdoors as much as I do, and she's not clingy." He smiled and gazed at the wall as if he were seeing the woman in front of him. "She's got one helluva great body, and kisses like nobody's business. I really think I'm in love with her." He glanced up at his brother. "I'm sure she's the one for me."

Tucker snapped his fingers, urging his brother to get to the point. "Name?"

"You know her. Hell, you've gone out with her a few times yourself." He grinned. "Molly O'Brien."

Lead sank to the pit of Tucker's belly, and his jaw tightened. "Sorry, she's taken."

Jake shot a frown toward his brother. "Well, damn. Did I miss something? Who snuck in and claimed her?"

Tucker stood, pushing his chair back so hard it hit the wall. "Me."

Jake's brows wrinkled. "You? When did you pop the question? Hell, I'm your brother. You could have at least consulted me before you did."

Tucker pulled at the collar of his Maddox Air Charter Service polo shirt and looked away from his brother's gaze. "It's not official yet."

"What do you mean it's not official?"

"Well…" Tucker's cheeks burned, "I haven't actually asked her. I planned to take her out over the next couple weeks, get to know her even better and let her get to know me. Then I'll pop the question."

Jake's frown lifted and his face split into a smile. "You haven't asked her?" He slapped his cowboy hat against his thigh. "Whew! And I thought she was a goner." He stood and plunked his hat on his head. "As far as I'm concerned, she's fair game until she says yes."

Tucker's eyes narrowed. "I've had my eye on Molly longer than you. Don't get in the way of my courtship."

Jake laughed out loud. "Listen to yourself. You sound like a man from the eighteen hundreds. Molly is young, daring and adventurous. Why would she marry a stick in the mud like you?"

"Any woman would be happy to marry a man who's stable, caring and treats her like she's special."

Jake yawned. "Boring."

Tucker slammed his fist onto the desk. "Damn it, Jake! This isn't a game or sporting event like when we were in high school competing against each other. I care about Molly. I'd go so far as to say, I'm in love with her."

"So am I." Jake's shoulders straightened, and he stared hard at Tucker. "I care enough to let her choose who she wants to be with. We both have a shot at winning her heart. We can date her and let her get to know both of us. After two weeks, she can make her choice and the one she doesn't choose has to back off."

Tucker thought about it for a minute. Molly was pretty independent-minded and would make her own decision. He just had to convince her to choose him. "Two weeks might not be enough for her to decide."

"Then we'll reevaluate at the end of the two weeks and extend the deadline if that's what it takes." Jake stepped up to his brother. "So for the next two weeks, we'll *both* date the pretty Molly O'Brien without interfering with each other's attempts to win her over." He stuck out his hand. "Deal?"

Not convinced this was a good idea, Tucker didn't have much choice. He took his brother's hand and shook on it. "Deal."

"Now, let's get out of here. I have some errands to run and then there's a beer with my name on it at the Ugly Stick."

"And I have some accounts to take care of back at the ranch." Tucker fully intended to ignore the accounts. To win Molly's heart, he had to get to her before his brother. If he wasn't mistaken, she worked at the Ugly Stick Saloon that night. He'd have to be there before Jake and stake his claim on the pretty lady, to let her know he was interested in long-term commitment.

Jake was as charming as a snake-oil salesman and could talk a girl out of her panties in the blink of an eye. Tucker would have his work cut out for him if he wanted Molly to fall for him.

"Molly!"

Molly O'Brien had just pulled on her boots and her cowboy hat after arriving home from a quick trip to town for groceries. "What do you need, Gabe?" she called out to her brother.

"Have you seen Isabella?" his voice came to her from the hallway.

Molly shook her head and smiled. "She's probably out at the barn with her horse."

"I checked. She and her horse were gone." Gabe stopped in front of Molly's bedroom door. "Where are you going?"

"It's hot outside. I've spent the best part of my day pushing a shopping cart through the grocery store, and I'm ready to blow the cobwebs out of my hair."

"Going riding, huh?" Gabe nodded. "That's what Isabella does when she's all wound up. What's got your chaps in a twist?"

"Nothing. Everything."

Gabe grinned. "You're talking like a female. Didn't we teach you better?" He crossed his arms over his chest and leaned against the doorframe. "Spill."

She shrugged and stood, stomping her foot to get it

the rest of the way into her boot. "I'm twenty-seven years old, I have a degree in marketing, I work at a saloon and I haven't gotten laid in the past six months. Either things better change around here soon, or I'm heading for Austin to find a job and men my age to date."

"There are plenty of men in Temptation who'd love to date you," Gabe said.

Molly lifted her chin. "Yeah? Name one."

"What about Nick...No, wait...I'm going to his bachelor party next week." Gabe scratched his jaw and frowned. "How about Grant Raleigh? He's a champion rodeo rider."

"Taken," Molly said. "Try again."

Gabe lifted two fingers. "Mark or Luke Gray Wolf."

"In a relationship with Libby Jones."

Gabe frowned. "Trent Jameson."

"He and Isaac are with Lucky Albright."

"Well damn, Molly. You're not trying hard enough." Gabe turned and led the way toward the kitchen. "There are more men around than that."

"I'm running out of options, and I'm not settling for some toothless old goat because I'm desperate." Molly's lips twisted. Not even a toothless old goat had asked her out in the last couple of weeks.

Gabe draped an arm around her shoulder. "I don't expect you to *settle* for anyone. Especially not an old goat."

"Well, in case you haven't noticed, the good ones aren't beating down my door to ask me out."

Gabe stepped back and stared at Molly in her jeans and tank top. "Why not? You're all right for a girl."

She snorted. "Thanks. I think."

"You know what I mean." Gabe scratched his head. "You being my baby sister and all."

Molly tilted her head, considering her dilemma. "I think the guys might be intimidated by my heavy-handed brothers."

"Whose heavy-handed brothers?" Sean entered the kitchen through the back door, followed by Tanner, his arm wrapped around Isabella's waist.

With three of the four hulking O'Brien men in the kitchen, it didn't leave Molly much room to move, much less think.

"Are you boys being overprotective again?" Isabella asked. She left Tanner's side and closed the distance between her and Molly. "Molly's a grown woman. She can take care of herself."

"What are you talking about?" Tanner asked. "She's just a kid."

"I'm twenty-seven. A year younger than Isabella."

Isabella slipped an arm around Molly and hugged her close. "She's fully capable of making her own decisions about men."

Molly smiled at Isabella's defense and gave a curt nod to her brothers. "That's right."

Sean frowned. "What if one of them tries to hurt her?"

"Yeah." Gabe's chest swelled. "We promised Dad we'd look out for our little sister. Speaking of Dad, he'd kick our asses if he comes home from his trip to Australia to find his baby girl moved out."

"First of all, if someone tries to hurt me, I'll take him down with one of the moves you taught me," Molly said. "Second. Dad isn't coming home for another month, what he doesn't know won't hurt him. Besides, you boys are too big for Dad to kick your asses."

Gabe's brows crooked upward. "You've seen him when he gets mad."

Molly shook her head. "The point is, I haven't been asked out on a date for a while. It might just be time for me to move on and make a life of my own away from Temptation where everyone knows everyone else."

"But Austin is such a big city," Gabe said.

"It's full of crime," Sean added.

Tanner frowned. "And far away."

"It's not as far as where Jesse lives," Molly pointed out.

Gabe's frown deepened. "Don't even think of running off to New York."

"I'm not going that far. Yet. But I *am* going to Austin, just as soon as I find a job. I've updated my resume, and I've signed up with a headhunter. It's time I grew up and got a life of my own."

All three of her brothers spoke at once, the combined noise too much to make any sense.

Molly raised her hand. "Don't bother trying to talk me out of it. I need to do this for me. There's nothing in Temptation holding me back." And no one begging her to stay.

"What about us?" Sean asked. "Don't you care about us?"

With a gentle smile for her brother, Molly touched his cheek. "I love you all, and Isabella too. You know how happy I am you've found each other. Seeing your loving relationship only makes me feel more alone."

"You're not alone," Tanner said. "You have us."

Molly shook her head. "You missed the part about my not having gotten laid in the past six months."

Tanner pressed his hands over his ears. "I did not want to know that."

"That I haven't been laid? Or that I'm not a virgin?" She backhanded him in the belly, forcing him to drop his hands.

"Either." Tanner closed his eyes. "I can't see my baby sister in bed with a man." He shook his head and glanced at her. "Sorry. I'll always see you as a ten-year-old."

"Exactly." She stared around at three of her four brothers. "As long as you three are around, I'll be an old maid. I'm giving Audrey my notice tonight. I'm giving myself two weeks to find a job, and then I'm out of here." She marched toward the door, pushing past Tanner.

"Wait!" Tanner snagged her arm. "What about those fly boys, Jake and Tucker Maddox?"

"Yeah," Sean said. "They aren't too old."

Her footsteps faltered at the thought of the Maddox brothers. Yeah, she liked them all right, had even thought she might be falling in love with them. She'd gone out several times with each and enjoyed the dates immensely, but neither had called her in more than two weeks. "What about them?" she hedged.

"I thought you liked one of them," Tanner said.

Sean added, "They're single."

Gabe grinned. "Best of all they're young, and have all of their teeth."

"Huh?" Tanner looked at his brother.

Gabe waved his hand. "Never mind. You ought to be able to catch one of the Maddox brothers."

Molly shook her head. "They aren't fish. I'm not going to throw a line in the water and snag one of them."

Isabella chuckled and rolled her eyes. "Molly, sweetie, good luck with these three poor excuses for matchmakers. I'm going to get a shower." She hugged her. "If you need an ear to vent in, come see me later."

Molly gave Isabella a grateful glance. "Thanks, Bella."

Fortunately all three of her brothers' attention swerved to their departing love, as Bella left the kitchen.

"Well, uh, I'm sure you'll figure it all out," Sean said to Molly, his gaze on Isabella's swaying hips.

"Yeah, Isabella's right—you're old enough to make your own decisions." Tanner pushed past Sean on his way after Isabella.

"Hey!" Sean grabbed his brother's arm and hauled him back. "The shower's only big enough for two."

"I know," Tanner said. "Isabella is one. I'm the two."

"Like hell you are." The two wrestled each other out of the kitchen and bumped into the walls down the hallway.

"I'm taking my shower alone," Isabella called out from the back of the house.

The men stopped fighting.

"What about after?" Sean asked.

"We'll see," Isabella's voice faded away.

Gabe pulled Molly into one of his big bear hugs. "Just don't rush into leaving. We love you and would like you to stay close to family. We've already lost one of us to the lure of the big city. We'd hate to lose you as well."

Molly squeezed her brother around the middle, burying her face in his shirt, loving the scent of the outdoors that reminded her so much of her father. "You didn't lose Jesse. He's alive and well, riding his horse for the New York City Police Department. And he's happy with the love of his life." She leaned back in her brother's arms and stared up at him. "That's all I want—to be happy with the love of my life."

Her brother tweaked her nose like he had when she'd been an eight-year-old. "I get that. But give the men of the area a chance before you bail on the ranch and us. That's all we're asking."

Molly sighed. "I'll give it until I find a job I can make a living at in Austin. If nothing happens by then, I'm packing my bags."

"Fair enough." He let his arms fall to his sides.

Molly nodded toward the hallway where Isabella, Sean and Tanner had disappeared. "You better hurry. The boys will wear her out before you get to her."

Gabe winked. "I can wait."

"Maybe you can, but can she?" Molly laughed. "I don't know how you four make it work."

Her brother ran a hand through his hair. "I don't either, but somehow it does. Who'd have thought the three of us could share one woman and not kill each other?"

Molly smiled, shaking her head. "I'm happy for you. Isabella is special. Don't screw it up." She left Gabe in the kitchen and headed out to the barn.

Little Joe stood at the pasture fence, waiting for her, stomping his hoof.

"You are so spoiled." Molly dug a carrot out of her pocket and held it out for the horse. She had to stop bringing carrots, apples and sugar cubes when she visited the barn. Little Joe had come to expect a treat every time.

She led the gelding into the barn, brushed and saddled him, and slipped a bridle over his head. By the time she was finished, he was dancing excitedly, as ready as she was to race across the pasture, letting the wind blow in his ears.

Outside the barn, Molly stepped into the stirrup and slung her leg over the saddle. She hadn't even gotten her foot in the other stirrup before Little Joe took off.

Laughing out loud, she let go of her worries, leaning over the horse's neck. She loved the feel of the hot sun's rays beating down on her back and the big, blue hazy sky of a Texas summer stretching above her.

Little Joe galloped across the fields, down into the valleys and up over the knolls, headed for his and Molly's favorite place in the whole world—the bend in the creek where a pool had formed. The place her parents brought her and her brothers when they were little and taught them to swim.

It was the one place on the entire ranch where she felt the most relaxed and comfortable. Away from everything and everyone, she could really think through her options...or not think at all.

Little Joe arrived at the creek, breathing hard, his coat lathered with sweat.

Molly swung off his back and dropped to the ground. She led the horse to the water and he drank, pulling gulp after of gulp into his mouth. When he was satisfied, he wandered toward a shady patch of grass where he happily munched.

Oh to be so easily satisfied. Molly sighed, toed off her boots and sat on a boulder at the pool's edge, dangling her feet in the cool water, watching the ripples spread out across the surface.

Gabe's words came back to her.

What about the Maddox brothers?

That was a question she had posed to herself a dozen times. She'd been around them for years, hanging out at the Ugly Stick Saloon. They'd danced together, and partied when the saloon had special events. Tucker and Jake were brothers, but as different as night and day.

Tucker was the levelheaded, sweet and considerate man a girl could see herself marrying. Oh, and he was an excellent kisser, and his slow, steady foreplay stirred her insides to the point where she'd wanted to strip naked and push him out of that sweet comfort zone. He'd only gone to second base, feeling up her breasts before he'd stepped away and ended the evenings they'd spent together. He wanted her to be sure about them before they went any further.

Yeah, he was sweet, and those big, rough hands...*Wowza*.

Now, Jake was the kind of man mamas warned their daughters about, and daddies stood at the front door with their shotguns to keep away. He made her core ignite. One of the dates she'd been on with him had ended abruptly when her brother, Tanner, drove up behind them at Lookout Point and put the kibosh on a backseat quickie. Yeah, her brothers had a habit of showing up at the wrong time.

And what killed her was that the dates had stopped a couple weeks ago. Neither Jake nor Tucker had called to claim another. And maybe that was a good thing. At some point, she'd have to choose between the two of them and she wasn't so sure she could.

Both men were professional pilots, driven in their desire to make their business work for them, and still cowboys at heart. She loved that about them and she was so close to falling in love with both of them, it scared her.

The thought of the two men made the day warmer to the point Molly pulled her tank top out of the waistband of her jeans and flapped the hem to stir up a breeze against her heated skin.

"Oh, what the heck." She yanked the shirt over her head and dropped it beside her on the boulder. The cool, clear water below beckoned. Within seconds, she'd shucked the rest of her clothes down to the bathing suit she'd been born with.

Deliciously naked, she dove into the water, the cool liquid caressing her hot body, bringing her outer temperature down while her core flamed. Nothing was better than skinny-dipping unless it was skinny-dipping with a really hot guy.

CHAPTER TWO

Jake was on his cell phone before he backed out of the parking lot, dialing Molly O'Brien's number.

"Hello?" a deep, male voice answered. Not unusual considering Molly lived with her father and older brothers. Jake had met them several times at the Ugly Stick Saloon. In a town as small as Temptation, you got to know just about everyone.

"Hello. May I speak to Molly?" Jake asked.

"Who's callin'?" the voice asked. Jake couldn't tell if it was Sean, Tanner or Gabe by his short responses.

"Jake Maddox."

"Maddox, you say?" A pause and a muffled yell. "Hey, Gabe, got a live one on the phone wanting Molls. What should I tell him?" Another pause and the brother came back on. "She's out at the barn gettin' ready to go for a ride. What do you want?"

Well, damn. If Molly went out for a ride up until the time she left for work, Jake would have to wait until that night and compete with Tucker for the lady's attention at the Ugly Stick. "I was hoping to catch her and see if she'd like to go out."

"Guess you'll have to ask her yourself."

"When will she be back?"

"Knowing Molly, not for a couple hours." Another pause and more yelling in the background. "He wants to ask her out!"

Jake stared at the phone in his hand wondering what the fuck was going on with the brother on the phone.

"If you want, you can come out to the ranch and wait for her." Pause. "Or you could take one of the horses and ride out after her. That is, if you haven't forgotten how to ride."

Jake bristled. "I ride."

"Good, 'cause she likes a man who can sit on a horse."

A thrill of excitement raced through Jake. Catching Molly out on the ranch would be perfect. They'd be away from her hulking brothers and even better, away from Tucker and everyone else. He'd have her all to himself. "I'll be there in fifteen minutes."

"We'll have a horse ready."

The Rocking O Ranch, where Molly lived with her brothers, was south of the Temptation Airport about ten miles. If Jake hurried, he might catch her before she rode out and they could ride together. After thirty minutes or so, he could find a nice place to stop in the shade and slip his arm around her. Maybe even steal a kiss or more.

Jake shoved his cell phone into his pocket, a grin spreading across his face. He'd get a head start on Tucker.

Breaking every speed limit between the airport and the Rocking O, Jake arrived in less than fifteen minutes.

The three O'Brien brothers rounded the side of the house, one leading a frisky gelding by the reins, fully saddled and ready to ride.

"If you head due west, you'll come to a hill." Gabe, the oldest of the O'Brien brothers, pointed across a pasture.

"Yup," Sean nodded. "At the top the hill, you'll see a valley dotted with trees. There's a creek running through it."

"Knowing Molly," Tanner handed the reins to Jake, "she's swimmin' in the creek. It's a hot day and the creek has a bend in it where a pool formed. She'll be there." Tanner winked. "Just look for the bend."

Tanner held the gelding's head while Jake, with a strange feeling he was being herded like a lamb to the slaughter, swung up in the saddle. Then he remembered Tucker would be pursuing the beautiful Molly just as hard as he was. If he could get in her good graces first, he stood a good chance of winning her over before his kind, considerate and boring big brother got his bid in for the prize.

Rather than look a gift horse in the mouth, Jake tipped his hat at the O'Brien brothers. "Thanks for the tip."

"Hey. Don't do anything we wouldn't do." Sean stood by a gate, holding it open for Jake to ride through. "And, believe me, we'd do a lot of things as long as the lady was willing."

Gabe strode up beside Sean and backhanded him in the belly. "Damn, Sean. We don't want him to think she's easy," he muttered beneath his breath, but not low enough Jake couldn't catch every word.

Again, he had that feeling he was being bamboozled. The brothers seemed eager to speed him on his way to their sister.

As Jake rode through the gate, he turned back to see Tanner, Gabe and Sean high-fiving.

What the hell was going on? The need to hurry while he had the chance of getting Molly alone drove further thoughts of her brothers out of Jake's head. He headed west across the pasture of new hay, shin-high and lush green.

The gelding, eager to be out in the open, broke into a gallop, its hooves gobbling up the distance. As mentioned, a hill rose up before Jake.

At the top, he gazed into a fertile green valley with a line of trees snaking down the middle.

Locating the bend in the line of foliage, he nudged the horse and rode down to a copse of brush and trees, anxious to kick off his plan to make Molly fall in love with him. Jake hadn't even entered the wooded area when he spied her horse, trailing his reins and munching on grass.

A stab of concern ripped through him. He slid out of his saddle and hurried toward her gelding. The horse raised its head, curious but not too interested in his approach, dipping his head back to rip up more grass with his teeth.

Speaking soothing words to the animal, Jake gave the horse a cursory check. No injuries, no scrapes or wounds. Which didn't mean anything. It could have been startled by a snake and thrown Molly.

His heart pounding, Jake dropped his own gelding's reins and pushed through the brush, emerging onto a flat, table-like rock. The boulder overlooked a broad pool of water, speckled with the sunlight glimmering through the canopy.

At first he didn't see Molly, which sent him to the edge of the rocky overhang, staring into the clear water, afraid of what he might find.

Instead of a corpse floating on the surface, he found a water nymph, skimming the surface, facing the sky, her eyes closed and her mouth curved in a smile, completely, incredibly, gloriously…naked.

Jake's groin tightened, and he stood for a moment staring down at the beauty, drinking in the lush curves of her body, the perky tilt of her breasts and the tight little budded nipples pointing skyward. *Holy hell.* His breath caught. The soft tuft of hair at the apex of her thighs had Jake's cock rock hard in an instant. He couldn't get out of his clothes fast enough.

He toed off his boots, jerked his company polo shirt over his head and shucked his jeans in record time. Soon, he stood naked, the gentle Texas breeze skimming across his skin and making him even more aroused.

Still, Molly floated, her eyes closed, her smile intact.

Jake almost hated to pull her out of the peaceful place she was in. A man driven by impulse, he couldn't just stand by and not touch the angel drifting in the water. He had to be near her.

What if she didn't want him in the pool with her? He'd kissed her a couple of times, touched her breasts and would have gone all the way at Lookout Point, if her brother hadn't shown up when he did. Jake thought they'd hit it off pretty well. Work had prevented him from pursuing her on a regular basis for the past month. Now that he had the time and the incentive to win her heart before his brother, he had to take the risk of surprising her.

He glanced around for the O'Brien men. Had they known their sister liked to skinny dip in the creek? Would they be waiting in the bushes with their shotguns loaded full of buckshot?

Jake covered his ass with his hands and squinted, checking the shadows. No movement other than the two horses happily chomping at the fresh grass.

Eyeing the water, Jake considered jumping in, but made the determination he'd be better off easing in and not startling the woman.

Padding to the edge of the boulder, he dropped down to the creek bank. As soon as his feet hit the cool mud, they slipped out from under him. He teetered on the edge of the water, knowing if he fell backward, he might hit his head on the boulder. Throwing his weight forward, he belly flopped into the water, landing near enough to douse Molly full in the face.

He went under, sucking a snoot full of water up his nose. Jake surfaced, coughing and cursing. By the time he was in control of his breathing again, he stared across at Molly, her arms crossed over her chest, her brows hiked.

"Some entrance." Her voice dripped sarcasm like her hair dripping a steady stream of water.

He grinned, coughed again and shrugged. "It was hot out. Would you believe I didn't see you?"

She shook her head, her lips twisting. "Not a chance. The question is, how long were you standing there before you fell in?"

He should have been ashamed of himself for spying on her...but he wasn't. "Not long," he fibbed. Long enough to see every delectable inch of her gorgeous body, but not nearly long enough to satisfy him for good.

Her eyes narrowed. "Uh huh. So you decided since you were here, and I was naked, you'd just join me without asking?"

Jake grinned. "I thought it might be easier to beg for forgiveness than for permission."

She nodded. "You're right. I would have told you to bug off."

"But since I'm here, and in the water, you don't have the heart to tell me to leave. Right?" He inched toward her.

Molly held up a hand. "I have brothers. You don't have anything different than what they have. But get one thing clear." She pointed a finger at his chest, close enough she could have touched him. "Hands off."

He held up his hand as if swearing on a bible. "I swear I won't touch you…" with a waggle of his brows, he added, "unless you want me to."

"Good. I'd tell you that I'd sic my brothers on you, but I don't need them to do my dirty work. I have a few of my own moves."

"Oh, yeah?" Jake's gaze drifted to the swell of her breasts rising above the water. He didn't have the heart, or the inclination to tell her that he could see her nipples beneath the surface. They were entirely too tempting, and he wished he hadn't made that promise to remain hands off unless she wanted him to touch her.

Jake sighed.

Molly's brows dipped. "Why the sigh?"

"I was thinking I'd have to convince you that you want me to touch me. Then I calculated how much time that should take. As far as I was concerned, it was minutes, hours, maybe even days, wasted." He waggled his eyebrows. "We could just cut to the chase."

Molly's laughter filled the little grotto of over-hanging trees like music on the wind. "Oh, sweetie, you'll have to work a lot harder than that." She pushed away from him, swimming toward the far edge of the swimming hole.

"Darlin', if I'm one thing, it's persistent. And I'm definitely up for the challenge." Oh he was up all right. And her saucy attitude only made him that much more determined to have her in his arms. He loved a sassy woman with spirit and drive.

Jake backed toward the shore, rising out of the water until he stood only waist-deep in a little patch of sunshine.

Molly stopped on the opposite side of the little pool, faced him and treaded water. "Are you going to swim?"

"I could use a little sun." He almost laughed at his lie. Jake spent a great deal of time in the sun, working on the ranch. The tan was natural and his toned muscles came from hard work, not a membership to a gym.

Molly's gaze swept over his chest and lower. Her eyes flared and the color in her cheeks brightened.

Jake flexed his muscles and grinned. "Like what you see?"

She shrugged, but she didn't look away.

Molly's hungry glance made Jake that much hotter, and more determined to push every last one of her erotic buttons. "I always say, if you know what you want, go for it."

"I don't want you," she said, her voice less convincing.

Jake swam after her, ducked beneath the surface and came up in front of her, only inches from her chest. "Are you sure?"

"Hey." She back-paddled, her eyes wide. "I said you couldn't touch me."

He held up his hands to show her where they were. "Not touching."

"I don't mind sharing the swimming hole, but you're crowding me."

"I promised not to touch you, unless you wanted me to." He rose out of the water, rivulets running down his chest. Where they were was only about waist deep for Jake. His cock bobbed near the surface, hard, thick and jutting toward her.

Her gaze followed the trickles of water streaming down his chest and lower, angling toward the juncture of his thighs and the rod just beneath the surface.

Jake could tell the moment she saw it. Her cheeks reddened and her eyes flared. Molly's tongue swept across her lips. "Are you always so…so…" she dragged her gaze up to his eyes, "…aroused?"

"Only around you, babe." He reached for her and caught himself before he put his hands on her arms. "Has anyone told you that you have a beautiful body?"

She crossed her arms over her chest again. "You shouldn't have been looking."

"You can't blame a guy for appreciating the natural beauty all around him. And darlin' you have a natural beauty all around you."

Her cheeks bloomed and her eyelids drifted closed for a moment. "Nice lines. Do you use them on all of your girlfriends?"

"I don't have a girlfriend. Yet." His gaze remained locked with hers. "But I'm working on it." He smiled, hoping to win her with the Maddox charm.

Molly's eyes narrowed. "Tell me something."

Jake spread his arms wide. "Anything."

"Why the sudden interest? We went out several times. I thought we'd made a connection, and then I didn't hear from you for the past two weeks. Why now?"

He tipped his head. "Fair question. My brother and I own a flying service. We go when our clients ask us to go. Word of mouth has spread and our business has had more work than we've ever had. We've flown days, nights and weekends for the past month."

"All work and no play…"

He puffed out his chest. "Exactly."

Her lips thinned. "I'm not interested in playing." She poked his chest with her slim finger. "I've seen you go out with every woman in the county. You're a player."

Jake raised his hands. "I'm a *reformed* player. Since we started dating, I haven't been out with another female."

Molly shook her head. "You just told me you haven't had time to date."

"I do now. And I want to date *you*." He inched closer, still not touching her, but barely.

Her eyes widened, and she caught her bottom lip between her teeth.

"Tell me the kisses we shared on our last date didn't mean anything." Jake held out a hand, praying she'd take it. He lowered his tone, making his voice more intimate. "Tell me you didn't want to go all the way at Lookout Point the last time we were together, and I'll walk away."

Her gaze shifted from his eyes to the hand and up to his mouth, the color in her cheeks deepening. "What does that prove?" she asked, her voice softening, her tongue sweeping out to moisten her lips. Molly dropped the arm covering her breasts and swirled the water, as if she wanted to touch him but didn't trust herself.

Jake's pulse quickened. "It proves there's something there. I felt it." He took a chance, scooped his hand beneath hers and lifted it out of the water. "You felt it, didn't you?"

She bit down on her bottom lip and nodded. "Yeah, but how do I know you aren't playing me?"

Jake carried her hand to his lips. "Give me a chance. I'll show you."

Her brows dipped, but she didn't pull her hand free. "I don't trust you."

"I can accept that. I have to prove to you I can be trustworthy." He stepped closer, his cock nudging her belly.

Molly's eyes widened. "We shouldn't..." She sighed. "I shouldn't..."

"But you're gonna..." He bent close enough he could kiss her, but far enough to make her come to him if she wanted it.

"Damn." She leaned up and brushed her lips across his. "I swore I wouldn't get tangled up with you."

He chuckled. "Didn't your mamma tell you it's not nice to swear?"

"Oh, shut up and kiss me." She wrapped her arms around his neck and pulled him against her body.

Inside, Jake rejoiced. Making love to Molly would be the start of his campaign to win her heart.

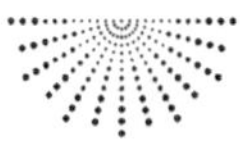

CHAPTER THREE

*H*oly *hell*. What was she doing? Molly's body was on fire as she slid skin-to-skin against Jake.

He ran his hand down her back, cupped her ass and lifted her. Buoyed by the water, she floated up to him, her legs naturally wrapping around his waist.

"This is so much more than a kiss," she whispered into his mouth, her brain telling her to stop. Her body ignored the hell out of her brain's repeated message—*Warning! This is a huge mistake!*

"Tell me to stop, and I will." Jake's voice slid over her like hot syrup on pancakes. "Although I don't know how I'll let go, when my body's telling me full steam ahead."

Though her brain was fuzzy with lust, Molly forced out the word, "Stop." She lifted her head, breathing ragged, pulse pounding, her control on the verge of crumbling.

Jake dragged in a breath and let it out, his body tense. "Change your mind?"

"Only if you tell me you don't have protection." She drew in a deep breath, her eyes closing, telling herself she'd done the right thing. "Please tell me you brought some?"

A grin slipped across his face. "I did. In my wallet. Hold on." Jake carried her across the pool to the rocky ledge where he'd watched her swimming. He stopped at the boulder and stood in water up to his hips.

Molly grabbed for the pile of clothing and dragged it toward her, desperate to find what they needed and get on with making love to the sexy, naughty cowboy.

She upended the blue jeans and Jake's leather wallet fell out, bounced off the rock and into the water.

"Damn!" Molly dove after it, forcing Jake to release her. It was just like her to be so clumsy. Not a sexy move at all, though it didn't diminish an ounce of the desire raging through her.

She surfaced, holding the wallet with a triumphant smile. "Got it."

Jake chuckled. "I didn't think you were that eager."

"I couldn't just jump your bones without it. A girl has to be a *little* hard to get." She fished in the wet billfold, snatched out the foil packet and tore into it with her teeth, tossing the wallet onto the boulder in a patch of sunshine.

"You do realize I don't want to date you just to get into your pants?"

Molly snorted. "Look, I'm going into this with really low expectations. I can't deny I want sex with you, but I'm not asking you to commit or anything."

His brow wrinkled. "What if I want the commitment?"

Molly's hand paused on its way to his jutting staff. "I'm not sure I want to commit to you or anyone." With a condom in one hand, his staff in the other, her thoughts shifted to another man. Jake's brother. Hell. Now wasn't the time to be thinking about another man.

Jake gripped her arms and held her steady. "I can't believe I'm saying this, but maybe we should forget about sex for now."

"What?" She stared at him, her mouth falling open. "Are you kidding me? I'm on fire, and you're getting cold feet?"

"Not cold feet. But making love to you means a lot to me."

"And it doesn't to me?" Molly's pussy clenched. "What if we aren't compatible in that respect?"

His brows lifted. "Not compatible? What do you mean?"

"What if we don't do it for each other?"

His hands still on her arms, Jake pulled her close enough for his cock to poke her in the belly. "Babe, you do it for me. I have no doubt about it."

Molly had come this far, committing to sex if not happily ever after. Surely that was enough. She wrapped her hands around his dick. "Tell you what. Let's test that theory and decide where we want to go from there." She rolled the condom over his hardness and fondled his balls. "Unless you want to forget all about it…"

Jake's head dropped back and he groaned. "I'm trying to be serious. I want more than just a poke in the pond."

"Oh, sweetie," Molly crooned. "Serious isn't your thing. Just poke me and let's see if we fit." With her hands braced on his shoulders, she lifted her legs, locked them around his waist and eased down until the tip of his shaft nudged her entrance. "Ready to find out?"

"Past ready," he said, his voice strained. "But we're not through talking."

"We are for now." Molly lowered herself over him, taking his full length inside her.

Jake was thick, hard and long, and he filled Molly so completely. Her head tipped back, and she moaned softly. "Oh, yes."

His hands slipped down to capture her ass, and he whispered against her ear, "I take it we fit."

"We do, and so deliciously." She tightened her

thighs, rising up.

Jake slid out of her almost all the way, paused, and thrust back into her, holding her bottom, to bury deeper the second time.

"Yes!" she cried. "Harder, darlin'! Faster!"

With his hands clamped around her butt cheeks, Jake slammed into her, splashing water up between them with the force of his thrusts.

Molly rode him, blood rampaging through her veins, her body tensing.

The faster he rocked in and out of her, the tighter her core grew and the more tense his muscles bunched beneath her fingertips.

One last thrust sent her spiraling over the edge. Tingling sensations, centering at her pussy, spread outward like lightning.

Jake's fingers dug into her ass, holding her hard against him, his body stiff. His shaft, buried deep inside, throbbed against the walls of her channel.

It felt so damned good, Molly almost forgot to breathe.

When she finally took a breath and let her body relax, she slumped against him, feeling as if she'd just run a marathon. "Well, that answers that question."

"What was the question?" he mumbled, the taut-ness of his muscles easing a little at a time.

"Do we fit?"

Jake nuzzled her neck below her earlobe. "Your verdict?"

"Oh, hell yeah." Molly leaned her head to the side to allow him better access.

"Does that mean you'll go out with me?"

She laughed. "That's a definite maybe."

"What more do I have to do to persuade you?"

Molly lifted his chin with her finger and pressed a soft kiss to his lips. "More of the same."

"Umm." He slid his tongue across the seam of her lips. When she opened to him, he caressed her tongue with his in a long, sensuous dance. "Give me a few minutes to recover."

Molly shook her head. "I don't mean right now, although I am tempted to go for a second round. I meant in the future. Sadly, I have to head back to the house and change for work. Audrey and the Ugly Stick Saloon need me tonight."

He caught her bottom lip between his teeth and pulled gently, letting it go before he spoke again. "I don't suppose you could call in sick?"

Molly sighed. "I can't. Audrey's pregnant and shorthanded. If I don't go in, she'll work the entire place by herself." She patted his shoulders. "I have to go. Let me down."

"Seems a waste to leave now when we've only just begun getting to know each other." Jake sighed. "But duty calls. Maybe I'll drop by for drinks."

"You should." She eased off his slackening cock and dropped her legs to the soft sandy creek bottom beneath her feet. "If you do, save me a dance."

"Save a dance? Oh babe, all my dances are saved for you."

Molly pulled herself up on the boulder and sat with her legs dangling over the edge. She wanted to believe Jake could be exclusive with her, but he had yet to prove it. Seeing him at the Ugly Stick Saloon with all the ladies around him would be a true test. He never seemed to be able to resist women.

TUCKER CHECKED himself over before leaving the ranch. Hair brushed. Check. Teeth brushed. Check. Best button-up shirt. Best jeans. Check. Check. His cowboy boots could use a coat of polish, but other than that, he looked passable.

He hoped like hell he'd get more than a passing glance from the beautiful Molly O'Brien. He could swear they'd hit it off the last time they were together. He hadn't imagined it. Since Jake would be at the Ugly Stick too, Tucker would have to get her alone to ask her out.

Speaking of Jake, the rumble of a truck engine alerted Tucker to a vehicle approaching the house. Jake had been gone most of the late afternoon.

Tucker walked out on the porch in time to see Jake step down from his truck and reach inside for his cowboy hat.

His brother's hair stood on end and his clothes were wrinkled and dusty.

Tucker frowned. "I thought you were coming straight home."

"Sorry." Jake's lips quirked upward on the corners for a brief second. Then he settled his cowboy hat on his head and climbed the stairs. "I had to take care of someone—something…first."

Tucker descended to the ground, passing Jake on his way up. "I'm headed out."

"Horses fed?" Jake asked.

"Yeah." Tucker snorted. "Thanks for being here to help. I thought you were going to the Ugly Stick."

Jake nodded. "I am, after I get cleaned up."

Tucker snorted and didn't offer to wait until Jake was ready. He wanted to take his own vehicle on the off chance he would be driving Molly home when she got off work.

Tucker patted his back pocket containing his wallet, with two condoms tucked safely inside. As he climbed into his pickup, he called out, "Feed the dog."

"Will do," Jake responded.

The drive to the Ugly Stick didn't take long and gave Tucker a chance to think. As darkness descended on Texas, he pulled into the parking lot of the saloon and stepped down from his truck. The sound of music from the jukebox vibrated the ground beneath his feet. Thursday nights at the Ugly Stick were rowdy, like the cowboys were just warming up for Friday nights. It was hardly conducive to wooing a woman who had to work the crowd, supplying drinks and food. He'd have to get her alone, the earlier the better, before the throngs of drunks took all of her attention.

At the sight of Molly's bright red Jeep Wrangler parked near the rear entrance, Tucker's pulse spiked. Tonight was the night he'd start his campaign to win her heart. She was the one for him. He'd known her a long time, liked the way she kissed and her happy, sassy attitude. Living with four older brothers, she was tough and no-nonsense, qualities he admired in a lady. And she was beautiful with her bright hair and bright green eyes.

Tucker loved the way she felt when her body pressed against his. His groin tightened. As much as he'd like to skip right to making love, he figured he'd better save that for after a date or two. She needed to feel comfortable around him and secure in the knowledge he was in it for the long haul.

His plan in mind, he entered the Ugly Stick Saloon, his gaze darting around the room. Fortunately he was early enough to take his pick of chairs.

"Evenin' Tuck." Greta Sue, the bar bouncer nodded as he passed her. The woman was as big as a linebacker and twice as tough. She should have been a prison guard, and maybe she had been in a previous life.

He considered asking the bouncer which tables

Molly was working, but decided against it. The big woman took her job seriously and looked after the waitresses working for Audrey Anderson.

Instead, Tucker crossed to the bar and slid onto a stool.

"What can I get you?" Libby Jones asked. The pretty, auburn-haired woman wiped the counter with a clean cloth, smiling his way.

"Bud Light, draft," Tucker answered, craning his neck, searching for Molly.

Libby filled a mug with his choice of beer and set it on the counter. "Looking for someone?"

"Is Molly working tonight?"

Libby nodded. "She's in the storeroom stacking cases of beer and whiskey, getting ready for tonight. Happy hour starts in thirty minutes."

Tucker lifted his mug and downed half of the clear, cool liquid in one long swallow. When he put down the mug, he stood. "I reckon I'll see if she could use a hand."

Libby's lips twitched. "I'm sure she could. Audrey's in the costume room, backstage with Jackson. They'll be no help for a while."

"At it again?" Tucker winked and crossed the floor. With the barroom half-empty and Molly alone in the storeroom, now was the most opportune time for him to make his move.

Since the storeroom door stood open, Tucker entered and searched for the bright-haired beauty.

A wall of beer cases stood dead center, blocking the view of the back of the room. Sounds of boxes being shifted and a few soft grunts drifted to Tucker. He leaned to the side of the wall of beer and caught a glimpse of a pert little ass, pointed skyward, encased in cutoff jean shorts, frayed at the edges and displaying more than a little of her rounded bottom. Long, silky legs stretched straight down to a pair of turquoise cowboy boots with a low heel and an elaborate design. She had bent to lift a case of Jack Daniels whiskey.

Tucker, hurried forward. "Hey, darlin', let me help you."

Molly squealed, popped upright and teetered backward with the box of whiskey.

Wrapping his arms around her, Tucker pulled her back against his front, holding her until she steadied.

"Damn it," Molly said. "Don't scare me like that." She stepped away from him and turned with the box.

Tucker grabbed the box from her hands.

"Tucker." Molly's cheeks reddened. "What are you doing back here? It's employees only."

"Libby said Audrey was busy and you might need help stacking cases."

Molly pushed her hair out of her face. "Actually I do. The delivery guy just dumped it all. I have to sort through and stack it in some kind of order."

"Tell me where you want it, and I'll put it there."

"Thanks." Molly glanced around him. "Are you alone?"

Tucker turned toward the door, a hot shaft of something akin to anger ripped through him. Jealousy? "Yes. Are you expecting someone?"

The color high in her cheeks, she shook her head. "No, no."

With Molly pointing, Tucker moved boxes. In a few short minutes, they had the boxes where Molly wanted them.

Molly stood with her fists on her hips and a smile. "That will keep Audrey from trying to do it herself."

Tucker frowned. "Surely she's not moving cases of booze still?"

With a laugh, Molly shook her head. "Not for lack of trying. Jackson follows her around like a shadow to keep her from touching anything heavier than a single glass of beer." A hair fell across her eyes. She swiped at it, leaving the cutest streak of dust.

But it was the sheen of perspiration across the swells of her breasts that nearly undid Tucker. His heart pounding against his ribs, Tucker took Molly's hand and carried it to his lips, brushing his mouth across her knuckles. "Molly, there's something I want to ask you."

Her clear green eyes stared up at him. "What's that, Tucker?"

"I'd like to take you out on a date."

Her brows lowered. "You've already taken me out

a few times and then you didn't call. Why should I go out with you after being ignored?"

He lifted her hand, weaving his fingers with hers. "I'm sorry about that. Business got heavy and I had some thinking to do."

She tugged on her hand, but he couldn't let go, afraid once he did, he'd never hold her hand again.

Molly sighed. "A phone call doesn't take that long."

"You're right." Tucker stared at where their hands met, electricity zinging through him at her touch. "I've spent the past couple of weeks thinking about what I want out of life, and who I want to spend it with." His gaze captured hers. "At the risk of moving too fast, I have to say...I want you."

She jerked her hand from his, her frown deepening, little lines appearing beside each side of her nose. "Me? Why?"

He missed the warmth of her hands, but couldn't help smiling. "That part was easy. I like that you are kind to everyone, whether they're being rude to you or not. I think you're cute as you wrinkle your nose when you're listening hard, like you are now."

Her frown lessened and the little wrinkle disappeared.

"I like that you're worried about Audrey and her pregnancy and that you love your family." He lifted her hand again. "And I like the way you kiss. I've been counting the minutes until I can do it again."

By the time he stopped speaking, her frown had

completely disappeared and her lips tilted upward, her eyes glistening. "That's about the sweetest thing anyone has ever said to me."

"I could go on, but it would delay the inevitable." He tugged her hand, drawing her closer.

"The inevitable?" she whispered, her body pressing against his.

"The inevitability of another kiss." He tilted her chin and bent his head. "That is, if you want me to kiss you."

"Oh, yes…" she whispered.

Before she could change her mind, Tucker swept in and sealed his intentions with a kiss, his mouth claiming hers in a gentle but firm connection. When she moved even closer, he traced the seam of her lips with the tip of his tongue.

Molly wrapped her hands around the back of his neck, weaving her fingers into his hair, then she parted her teeth, allowing his tongue to sweep the length of hers in a long, sensuous caress.

By the time Tucker lifted his head, his jeans were so tight they were strangling his cock.

Her breathing a little ragged, Molly leaned her forehead against his chest. "Just when I know what I want, a Maddox walks in and throws me off center."

He chuckled. "I'd say I'm sorry, but I'm not. I've done nothing but think about kissing you just like that."

She lifted her head and stared him straight in the

eyes. "Is that all you've been thinking about?" Molly eased closer until her belly rubbed against the hard evidence of Tucker's desire. "Just kissing?"

Lust ripped through him like a wildfire. He couldn't move too fast or he might scare her off. But he couldn't lie, either. "No. I've been thinking about holding you in my arms…" *Here goes.* "Beautifully and utterly naked." His breath caught and held.

Molly's green eyes darkened and her hand ran down his arm and around to caress his backside. "So all you've been thinking about is kissing me and holding me naked?" She pressed her hand against his buttocks until his cock fit snug against her belly. "Just holding?"

He swallowed the moan rising in his chest. The depth of his lust was so great, he fought to keep from tearing off her clothes and taking her there. "Darlin' what do you want me to say?"

"The truth."

He nodded. "Fine. I want to hold you naked and make hot, passionate love to you in every way I know how." Just the words make his dick so hard it hurt.

Molly's widened and she gave a strained laugh. "Was that so hard to admit?" She shook her head. "All I wanted was to know what it is you really desired."

"I'm willing to wait until we've dated for a while… give you a chance to get to know me and my level of commitment and loyalty."

She pressed a finger to his lips. "Shh. The way you

describe yourself you could be my dog. If you want to make love to me...do it. Now. Here in this storeroom."

He leaned back, his pulse beating a tattoo against his throat. "What do you mean?"

She walked to the storeroom door, shut it and locked it. When she turned to face him, she grabbed the hem of her tank top and pulled it up over her head.

Tucker raised his hands as if in surrender. "Darlin', are you not afraid someone might walk in?"

Molly stalked him like a lioness after her prey. "I'm too hot to care." She tossed her hair over her shoulder. "What if I want to make love to you immediately?"

"I want you to get to know me." Tucker backed a step.

"Fine, tell me about yourself, while I get naked." She unclipped her bra and let it slide down her arms. Pert breasts with the prettiest rosy nipples bounced free.

Words got stuck in Tucker's throat. He hadn't planned for her coming on to him and he didn't know how to react. "I'm loyal," he stumbled.

"You already said that. My dog is loyal and you're not making me horny with that kind of talk." She toes off a boot. "Tell me something personal."

"Like what?"

She grinned and took off the other boot. "Boxers or briefs?"

"Neither."

"Now you're talking." Her voice lowered and her glance dipped to his crotch. "Show me."

"Now?" Heat rose up his chest, seared across his face and out to his ears. "In here?"

"Now." Her brows hiked in challenge. "Here." She reached for the button on her cutoffs and flipped it free. "I'll show you mine, if you show me yours." Her hand stilled on the zipper, and she tilted her head. "Unless you're too shy. In which case, you might as well go home." Molly started to button her jeans.

Tucker reached out to stop her. "Don't."

"I want a man who knows what he wants and isn't afraid to go after it."

"I love that about you." He pulled her close and inhaled the scent of herbal shampoo. "I'm not afraid of going after what I want. I was more afraid of being too forward and scaring you off. But if you want it here and now...by all means." He set her to arm's length, yanked his button free of the hole and jerked down the zipper. His cock sprang free, hard, straight and aching to be inside her.

Molly smiled and curled her hand around his erection. "Now was that so hard?"

"Darlin', it's hard, all right." He narrowed his eyes. "Now, what are you going to do with it?"

Her smile widened. "I didn't think you had it in you."

Tucker gripped her arms. "I have it and more where you're concerned. If you want to make love in the storeroom of the bar, I'm game."

She ran her hands across his chest, one sliding lower to cup his cock. "I thought you were the by-the-books kinda guy, afraid to step outside of your comfort zone."

He forced a shrug, though his body tensed, the source of the tension being fondled by her soft but firm fingers. "I fly planes. Each time I leave the ground I step outside my comfort zone."

Molly reached lower, her fingers curling around his balls. Molly leaned up on her toes and whispered in his ear, "Then why do you do it?"

He turned and captured her lips with his in a hungry kiss before pulling back to answer. "Because I love it."

When he'd taken his introductory flight, Tucker knew instantly he wanted to be a pilot. With Molly, Tucker had known at their first kiss she was the woman for him. When he committed to something he was passionate about, there was no stopping him. Winning Molly's heart was his next goal. Tucker wouldn't settle for less.

"Umm." Molly flicked the buttons on Tucker's shirt with her free hand while rolling his balls in her other. "I love a passionate man. It makes me want to fuck him wherever I am."

Tucker chuckled. "Does your daddy know you use that kind of language?"

"My daddy is in Australia and still thinks I'm a virgin." Her hands moved back to his staff and wrapped around him. "And you're killing the mood by talking about him."

"Whatever the lady wants." Tucker backed her up against a stack of boxes, dug his fingers into her hair and tugged. The motion tipped her head back, exposing her long, sexy neck. He nipped her earlobe and trailed a line of kisses and nibbles down to the pulse beating rapidly at the base of her throat. "One thing..." he said, flicking his tongue across the throbbing vein.

"One thing?" she asked, her voice breathy, hitching.

"I'm not after a one-night stand or just a quickie in the back room." He cupped the back of her head with both hands and stared into her green eyes, knowing he could wake up to her face every day for the rest of his life. "I want you in my life, not just in my bed."

Her green eyes, glazed with desire, blinked. "What if I'm not ready to commit?"

Tucker smiled. "Then I'll just have to change your mind, won't I?" He reached for her zipper and dragged it down. "I can be very convincing."

olly's breath escaped on a soft gasp and she caught her bottom lip between her teeth. She couldn't get her shorts off fast enough. The added danger of being caught by one of the staff or the boss was so titillating she nearly came before she was fully disrobed.

Tucker helped, sliding the garment over her hips and down her legs, his hands gliding over her skin, making every inch tingle along the way.

When the shorts pooled at her ankles, she stepped out and stood before him, naked and ready for more.

Part of her felt guilty for making love to his brother only hours ago. Molly tried to tell herself, it was just sex, but in her heart she didn't believe it. Then again, she hadn't committed to either and had told them as much. Therein lay her problem. She couldn't decide which brother she liked better. Hopefully, by sampling each, she could come to a decision. Lovemaking could be a deal-breaker, if the man wasn't in tune with her desires.

Tucker bent, scooped her up by the backs of her legs and sat her on a stack of boxes. "Are you sure about this? I could take it slower." He winked.

Dear Lord, if he went any slower, she'd spontaneously combust.

"I'm sure." Molly parted her knees and ran her hand over her belly to the tuft of hair at the apex of her thighs.

When she dug her fingers into her folds, Tucker's eyes flared.

If Molly wasn't mistaken, he wanted her as badly as she wanted him, and by playing with herself, she might just move things right along.

Tucker tipped her head back and claimed her lips in a deep, soul-defining kiss. From there, he kissed his way over her chin, down her neck and across to her perky right breast. He captured her nipple between his teeth and rolled it, tonguing and flicking it until it tightened into a hard little bud.

Her nerves on fire, every cell in her body hopping with energy and desire, Molly arched her back, laced her fingers into the hair at the back of his head, and urged him to consider the other breast.

Moving to the left, he toyed with her other nipple until it matched the first—tight, hot and deliciously achy.

A moan escaped Molly's throat.

Tucker was good. So very good. But she wanted more.

"Enough of the breasts," she cried, guiding his head farther south.

Tucker dropped to one knee and ran his hands along the insides of her thigh, searing a path toward her center.

Yes! A little closer, please.

She clasped the back of his head, arching toward him as he kissed and licked his way down to the juncture of her thighs.

She wiggled her bottom, scooting toward him, eager for him to claim her there.

When he parted her folds with his big, calloused thumbs, she nearly cried with relief.

Then all thoughts flew with one touch of his big, coarse finger, stroking the length of her clit.

Holy hell, it felt so good. "Again," she breathed.

His finger touched her at the top and slowly dragged down the length of her nubbin and lower to her damp pussy. Tucker thrust in and swirled, another finger dipping down to the tight round pucker of her anus.

Molly tensed, her body on fire, her senses on overload.

He wouldn't.

Tucker pressed in at the same time as he touched her clit with the tip of his warm, wet tongue.

"Oh, dear Jesus!" She nearly came off the stack of boxes, the intensity of the electric shocks shooting through her almost more than she could bear. And yet, it wasn't enough. She wasn't sure she could ever get enough of Tucker's tongue on her.

Sucking her clit into his mouth, Tucker tongued and flicked over and over.

Molly's fingers wove into his hair and pulled, as Tucker swirled, touched and stroked.

One more flick and she launched into the stratosphere, her body pulsing with her release, fireworks bursting inside and shooting outward to the very tips of her extremities.

For a long moment, she didn't breathe, riding the waves of her orgasm to the very end.

When she finally drifted back to earth, she pulled on his hair, dragging him to his feet. "Now. Inside. Please." She couldn't say any more than that, her lungs burning to catch up. Though she'd come, she wouldn't be completely satisfied until Tucker thrust his hard dick into her, filling her until she could feel no emptiness.

Still wearing his jeans, Tucker reached into his back pocket and withdrew a foil packet.

Molly snatched it from his fingers and tore it open.

He chuckled. "In a hurry?"

"Hell, yeah." She tossed the packet aside and rolled the condom down over him. Then she gripped his hips and guided him to her wet entrance. "Now, fuck me like there's no tomorrow."

Tucker brushed a quick kiss across her lips, grabbed her hips and thrust into her, burying himself all the way to the hilt, his balls slapping her anus.

"Yes!" she cried. "Again."

He pulled out and rammed into her with another thrust, deep, hard and thoroughly satisfying. Tucker settled into a rhythm, driving in and out like a piston, smooth, slick and thick.

The friction set her senses climbing up another peak.

Molly fingered her clit, pressing hard against the nubbin as she flew over the edge yet again.

Tucker thrust one last time and remained buried inside her, his hands tight on her ass, fingers digging in as he came. His cock throbbed against the walls of her channel, pulsing and heated and oh, so very big.

"Wow." Molly drew in a deep breath and let it out. "You sure have a way of convincing a girl."

"You inspire me to greatness." He kissed her, his tongue thrusting past her teeth to take hers.

The taste of her musk in his mouth made Molly want to do it all over again.

A sharp knock jerked Molly out of the lust-induced cocoon she'd been in and back into the musty, dark interior of the bar's storeroom.

"Molly?" Audrey's voice called out through the hardwood panel. "Are you all right in there?"

"Yes," Molly said, her voice nothing more than a croak. She cleared her throat and tried again. "I'm fine. I'll be out in a minute."

Reluctant to break their connection, Molly glanced up at Tucker. "I have to go back to work."

"Dance with me later?"

"Yes." Heat filled her chest and rose up into her cheeks as Molly remembered promising Jake the same. Fuck! She was no closer to deciding which man she liked better. They both were hardworking, gorgeous, with big hands, and each man had his...skills.

Another knock at the door made Molly jump.

"If you need any help, Jackson and I can join you," Audrey said. The sound of a giggle could be heard. "Stop that Jackson. You had your turn in the props room."

Tucker pushed into her a little, then slipped all the way out. "We better unlock the door before they use a key." He peeled off the condom and dropped it into a trashcan.

"Here, let me." Molly reached behind her, grabbed a roll of paper towels from a shelf and tore off a square. She gently wiped the come off him and tucked his cock back into his jeans. "For the record...that was incredible."

He zipped and grabbed the roll of paper towels. "My turn." He parted her legs and patted her pussy dry.

Which only inspired her to want more. Finally, she covered his hand, her core so hot, she couldn't take it anymore. "If you keep that up, I'll have to let Audrey and Jackson in to participate."

His widened and a sexy smile tugged at his lips. "You'd do that?"

"I'm not the sweet little innocent my brothers think I am. Hell, I have to listen to all three of them banging Isabella every night. You want to talk about expanding my imagination? That'll do it. It's no wonder my father decided to visit a ranch in Australia for three months."

Tucker's chuckle warmed the air around Molly. "It's an interesting concept. I wonder how the four of them pull it off." He lifted her off the stack of boxes and set her on her feet.

"They all love her and she loves all of them equally." Molly pulled her shorts on and reached for her bra. "You'd think it would be a mess, but they make it work."

Tucker's brows dipped. "I think I'd have a hard time sharing you with anyone." Before she could hook her bra in place, he pulled her into his arms. "You're an amazing woman."

Molly rested her hands against his chest and voiced what was on her mind, "What if I want what Isabella has?"

"More men?" Tucker leaned back. "I don't know..."

"Not like an open-ended relationship where I

could be with as many men as I wanted, but maybe with one other guy. You both could share me."

Tucker stiffened. "I'm not into doing it with another guy."

Molly shrugged. "You wouldn't have to. You could both be doing me, not each other."

His brows dipped low. "I've never considered it. It's not my style."

She patted his chest. "Think about it. If you really want to keep me around, you might have to compromise. I might like the option of multiple orgasms a night. Are you up to that?"

His chest puffed out. "Given a little time between."

Another knock on the door, cut into the conversation.

"Molly? I need a couple cases of Coors Light in the cooler, chilling," Audrey said.

"I really have to go." Molly pulled her bra straps up her arms, tugged her tank top over her head and shoved her feet into her boots. She hated leaving him with that confused and frustrated look on his face, but she had to get back to work. Standing on her tiptoes, she brushed her lips across his.

Tucker grabbed her around the middle and kissed her hard. "You ask a lot of a man."

"I know what I want, and I go after it." She slipped free of his arms and hurried toward the door. When she opened it, Audrey and Jackson fell inside.

Audrey glanced from Molly to Tucker. "Every-thing all right?"

Molly tossed her head toward Tucker. "Ask *him*." She grabbed a case of Coors Light and left the store-room before Tucker could respond.

Damn, she'd more or less given Tucker an ultima-tum. Share her with another man or lose her. Shit. Wait until he realized the other man was his brother!

JAKE TOOK HIS TIME SHOWERING, feeding the dog and dressing for his night at the saloon. If men glowed after sex, he was definitely glowing inside. His deci-sion to pursue Molly O'Brien was the right one. Now that he'd made love to her, he was even more certain than before he couldn't live without her.

She was smart, spunky and daring. Being openly sensual on top of all that made it a no-brainer. Molly was the woman for him, and he got there ahead of Tucker. He almost laughed with his happiness.

For a very short moment, Jake felt bad for his brother. But not bad enough to back off and let Tucker have Molly. Molly was perfect for Jake in every way.

He dressed in his best blue chambray shirt and jeans, pulled on his favorite cowboy boots, shined his rodeo buckle and topped it all off with a black Stetson.

Jake Maddox was ready to see the woman he considered his destiny. A couple more nights with Molly and he might even consider popping the question.

Hell, he needed to find the right ring before he did that.

As he hurried toward his pickup, he reined in his thoughts. First things first. He had to get her to commit to him. She'd been pretty vague on the subject earlier.

The drive to the Ugly Stick felt longer than usual. Wanting to see Molly was foremost in his mind. Catching her in the storeroom would be a helluva bonus—if he got lucky, and the woman was willing. Audrey and Jackson made a habit of doing it in the storeroom, or in the costume room back stage. He'd walked in on them once, and they'd invited him to stay and watch. He had. It had been one of the most erotic things he'd ever done. One he wouldn't soon forget.

Those two couldn't get enough of each other. After one time with Molly, Jake understood their desire to make love anywhere and everywhere they could.

The parking lot of the Ugly Stick was jammed full of pickups and SUVs. The music blared so loudly it seemed to shake the tin sides of the building.

So much for catching Molly in the storeroom. She'd be too busy for a quickie.

Jake sighed. He'd just have to wait and take her home with him. He could be patient...when the wait was worth it. Molly was worth it.

He spied Tucker's truck next to the front entrance. He must have gotten there before the crowd descended. Had his brother made a move on Molly in the short time he'd been there?

Jake was forced to park a long way from the door in the overflow field. He didn't mind. It gave him a few more minutes to think about Molly's naked body floating in the water.

Inside the saloon, Jake weaved his way through the throng to the bar, craning his neck, searching for Molly. He spotted her waiting a table on the far side of the room. There were no spare chairs at any of her tables or at the bar for that matter. Jake sidled up to the counter and waited to catch Libby's attention.

The bartender had her hands full of mugs, filling them as quickly as she could from the Budweiser tap. One at a time, she set them on a tray until it was full. Adding a bowl of pretzels she looked up. "It's ready."

Charli, Audrey's assistant manager grabbed the tray, lifted it to her shoulder and headed into the fray.

Libby filled a mug for Connor Mason who sat at the bar watching Charli weave through the crowd.

Finally, Libby turned to Jake with a smile. "What can I get you?"

"Bud on tap," Jake said, and turned to watch Molly work her way to the bar.

Libby slapped his drink on the counter as Molly arrived with a tray of empties and her order for more drinks.

"Hey, beautiful," Jake said over the roar of the band on stage.

Molly glanced up and smiled. "Oh, hey, Jake. When did you get here?"

"Just now." He lifted his drink and sipped before continuing, "I came for that dance you promised."

She grimaced. "It's crazy tonight. I doubt I'll get a chance to get out on the floor."

"I can wait until it's not so busy."

She gave him a quick smile. "That might be a while." She lifted the tray Libby had filled with her order and headed out, long dark hair hanging down her back and hips swaying as she navigated through the crowded room.

Jake couldn't wait to get his hands on those hips again. Damn, she was sexy.

"I thought you'd be right behind me. What took you so long?"

Jake turned to find Tucker sitting two seats down from him, a big cowboy in between them. Funny how he hadn't noticed his brother until Tucker said something.

Jake stepped around the big guy and stood beside Tucker, his gaze on Molly. "I wasn't in a hurry."

"Still thinking Molly's your gal?" Tucker asked, his lips quirking on the corners as though he had a secret.

Jake's eyes narrowed but he answered, "Yup."

"I wouldn't be so sure."

"You know something I don't?"

His brother shrugged. "Just sayin'."

Jake stiffened. "Spill."

Tucker lifted a mug of beer. "I don't kiss and tell." He swiveled on his bar stool, facing Molly. "But, if I'm not mistaken, she's definitely interested in me."

Jake's stomach tightened and his fist clenched around the handle of his mug. "What do you mean?"

"Nothin'." Tucker shot him a look that said anything *but* nothing.

"What the hell—" Jake started but was cut off by the screech of a microphone.

Audrey stood on the stage in front of the band, smiling. "Gentlemen, give it up for the lovely ladies of the Ugly Stick Saloon!"

The band played the song *Save a Horse, Ride a Cowboy,* and all four waitresses working the saloon climbed onto the stage and danced, kicking up their heels in unison and shaking their asses like nobody's business.

By the time the music ended, Jake had a hard on. He set his mug on the counter and pushed his way through the crowd toward the ladies.

Connor was there to help Charli off the stage and

into his arms for a slow dance. Ed Judson swept Kendall Mason off her feet and swung her onto the dance floor. Nick McBride helped Lacey Lambert down.

Jake couldn't get around Nick and Lacey as they stumbled, laughing.

When he finally managed to step aside, Jake's stomach hit bottom.

Tucker had Molly by the waist, lifting her off the stage and into his arms. She slid down his chest, her arms curling around his neck until her feet touched the hardwood floor.

Fuck!

The band kicked off a slow dance and more couples crowded onto the floor.

Jake stood in the middle of them, without a woman in his arms, a scowl pulling at his face.

As Tucker waltzed Molly around, he shot a triumphant smile at Jake.

His fists clenched into a knot, Jake gave Tucker two turns around the floor before he marched over to the pair and tapped Tucker's shoulder. "I'm cuttin' in."

When Molly stepped back, Tucker shook his head and pulled her into his embrace. "No way. She's mine."

Molly's lips thinned, and she stopped in the middle of the dance. "Whoa there. I'm not yours, Tucker Maddox. I'm my own person."

Tucker glared at Jake, and then turned to Molly with a softer look. "I'm sorry," he said through clenched teeth. "You're right. No one owns you. Please, let's dance."

She shook her head. "When someone cuts in, the polite thing to do is let him take the dance. Didn't your mama teach you manners?" Molly held her arms out to Jake and gave Tucker a stern look. "Remember what I said earlier?"

Tucker's brows puckered. "About what?"

"Sharing?" she prompted. When Tucker's frown deepened, Molly snorted. "Never mind." She smiled at Jake. "Let's dance."

Jake swept her away, the feeling his brother was shooting daggers with his eyes into his back making him twitch. "What was that all about?"

"What?" Molly smiled, though her expression appeared strained.

"What did you mean by sharing?"

Molly's smile slipped and she stared up into Jake's eyes. "Let me pose a hypothetical question to you?"

"Okaaaay," Jake said, uncertainty making his steps falter. "Shoot."

She let him dance her around the floor once before continuing. "What if the woman you care about wants you as well as another man?"

Before she finished speaking, Jake shook his head. "It won't work."

Molly stopped in the middle of the dance and fisted her hands on her hips. "Why?"

"I'm a one-woman man. One woman. Not one-woman and a man." He reached for her hands. "Let's finish this dance."

"Jake Maddox, I'm serious." She shook free of his hands. "Three of my brothers found a way to share one woman between them. Why can't one woman share two men? That's one less man in the picture."

"Frankly, I don't know how your brothers do it." Jake ran a hand through his hair. "Wouldn't she get tired of all three of them?"

"As a matter of fact, she couldn't choose between the three, and it keeps the sex fresh when she has it with three different men." Molly crossed her arms over her chest. "If you're not up for a ménage a trois, there's no point in continuing this relationship."

Jake glanced around at the couples happily circling the dance floor, staring at him and Molly stalled in the middle. "I've never been in a ménage-a-whatever. Who did you have in mind as the third?"

Molly opened her mouth, but before a word could come out, Tucker was there beside her, anger pouring off him like fumes from a diesel truck.

"You've got to be kidding," Tucker said to Molly. "You can't be serious." He jerked his thumb toward Jake. "Him?"

Molly's lips pressed together and she nodded. "Yes."

Tucker shook his head. "No way."

Jake stared from Molly to Tucker and back to Molly, an inkling blossoming into a full-fledged understanding of what the two were arguing about. Jake pointed to Tucker. "You want the two of us to share you?"

Molly's chin lifted. "That's right."

Jake shook his head and echoed Tucker's words, "No way."

"We can barely share the business, how in the hell do you expect us to share a woman?"

The people dancing around them slowed, their attention captured by the three of them shouting in the middle of the dance floor. Molly glanced left and right. "You two chew on it. But I can tell you now-- I'm not going to choose between you. It's both or neither."

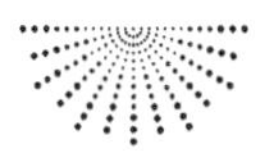

CHAPTER FIVE

Tucker glared at Jake. "What did you do to her?"

"Me?" Jake threw out an arm. "What did you do? I had her in the palm of my hand when we made love this afternoon."

"You made—" Tucker sputtered. "This afternoon? Busy taking care of something, huh?" He stepped around Molly and planted a hand in Jake's chest and shoved.

"Don't push me, Tuck," Jake warned. "You're older, but not a better fighter."

"You knew I had plans for this evening." Tucker pushed him again, anger building with each breath he took. "And you went behind my back."

"Based on Molly's demands, you had your chance as well." Jake shoved Tucker. "Let her choose, you said."

"That's right, and all you did was make it where she didn't want to choose." Tucker pushed Jake again.

Jake swung his fist at Tucker's jaw.

Tucker turned in time so that Jake's fist connected with his shoulder, pain radiating throughout his shoulder and arm.

Tucker balled his fist and landed one in Jake's gut.

Jake doubled over and came up swinging.

The female dancers scattered for the sidelines while the men formed a circle around Jake and Tucker and the betting began.

"Twenty on Tucker to win."

"Fifty says Jake will take him!"

Greta Sue shouted from the side of the dance floor. "Take it outside!"

Tucker wasn't taking anything. He landed an upper cut to Jake's jaw, sending him staggering backward into Ed Judson's arms.

Ed threw him back into the ring, laughing. "Take him Tucker. I got money on you."

Jake came back swinging and hit Tucker in the side of his mouth, splitting his lip. Blood spouted from the injury, only seeming to make Tucker madder. He swung again, but Jake ducked and hit him in the belly again.

Greta Sue hooked Jake with one arm and Tucker with the other and plowed them toward the door. People leaped out of the way, shoving chairs and tables out of Greta Sue's path.

Jackson Gray Wolf stood at the entrance to the Ugly Stick Saloon, laughing as he held open the door.

Greta Sue shoved Tucker outside and then Jake after him.

Jake crashed into Tucker as he scrambled to his feet and the two of them rolled across the ground, trading punches, kicks and flailing swings.

When they rolled into a ditch, Tucker sat back on his haunches, gasping for breath, his jaw numb from too many hits and his eye swelling.

Jake didn't look much better.

The crowd of men stood at the top of the slope cheering, until a siren's wail sounded from the highway.

Too tired to take another swing, Tucker lumbered to his feet, offering his hand to his brother.

Jake shoved it aside and tried to get to his feet, crashing to the ground when his legs wouldn't hold him.

"Take my damned hand," Tucker said.

Jake glared at his brother and took his hand. "I'm not finished yet." He bent over, his sides heaving. "Just give me a minute."

"Show's over," Sheriff's Deputy Dusty Cramer called out, pushing his way through the onlookers. "Tucker, Jake, what the hell's goin' on?"

"Not a goddamn thing." Tucker spit blood on the ground.

Dusty turned to Jake. "Jake, you want to fill me in?"

"Fuck you."

Dusty extended a hand to him.

Jake took it and pulled himself out of the ditch.

The crowd of men retreated, headed back inside for another round of whatever they were drinking.

Dusty helped Tucker out of the ditch. "Either one of you want to press charges?"

"No," Jake said.

Tucker shook his head. "Not this time."

"Any damage inside?" Dusty pulled a notepad out of his pocket. "I gotta write you up if there's any damage."

"Only to my face." Tucker touched his lip and winced.

"And my ribs." Jake pressed a hand to his side and bent over in pain.

"What's got into you two?" Dusty asked. "I haven't seen you go at each other since we were kids on the playground."

Jake didn't answer

Neither did Tucker.

"They're fighting over a woman." Greta Sue joined Dusty, her arms crossed over her chest. "No damage to the saloon or anyone inside."

"Well, then, I'll just go say hello to Audrey and grab a drink." Dusty gave Jake and Tucker the look. "Talk it out. Fighting settles nothing."

With those parting words of wisdom, Dusty followed Greta Sue back to the bar.

Jake flipped Dusty the bird.

"I saw that," Dusty called out from the door to the saloon, a grin spreading across his face.

Alone, Tucker glanced at the door, debating whether or not to go back inside and apologize to Molly and Audrey for raising a ruckus. But he looked like hell and Molly's words still echoed in his mind. "She wants us to share her," he said out loud.

"No fucking way." Jake shoved a hand through his hair. "She's mine."

"Not from what she said inside. She doesn't belong to anyone. Not you. Not me."

"Unless we choose to share her between the two of us." Jake let out a long breath. "Impossible."

"Damn right." Tucker agreed with his brother for the first time that night. "So what are we going to do?"

"Give her time to come to her senses?" Jake offered.

Tucker wasn't so sure that was a good idea. "What if she ditches both of us?"

"Would you rather see her with another guy than with me?"

"Hell, yeah," Tucker responded. Then thought about it and added. "Oh, hell no."

"I'd rather not lose her." Jake stared at the saloon. "She's special."

"Incredible." Tucker stared at the saloon too, as if he could see Molly through the walls.

"And she's got a body that doesn't quit," Jake continued.

Tucker spun and faced his brother. "So what the hell were you doing this afternoon? You went to see her without telling me, didn't you?"

Jake nodded, a grin spilling across his face. "She'd gone out riding. Her brothers met me at the truck with a horse, saddled and ready to go." Jake scratched his chin. "They seemed eager for me to follow her."

"So you did." Tucker's jaw tightened. "I should have known you'd jump in front of me. If you hadn't gone after her this afternoon, Molly would be all mine now. We made love in the storeroom before you got here."

"We did it in the creek, in front of God and the horses."

A jolt of jealousy hit Tucker in the gut, but he hurt too bad to react. "What are we going to do?"

"Go back inside and try to talk sense into her." Jake hitched up his jeans and ran his hand through his hair again.

"She has to choose." Tucker fell in step beside him and let Jake enter the saloon ahead of him.

The band had taken a break, but the jukebox was blaring and the dance floor was full of two-steppin' cowboys and cowgirls.

"Where's Molly?" Tucker squinted, his gaze

sweeping across the faces around the tables and to the bar. Molly wasn't anywhere he could see.

Jake nudged him. "There." He pointed to the dance floor.

Molly was in the arms of Deputy Sheriff Dusty Cramer, laughing and smiling like he hung the moon.

"Well, damn," Tucker said.

Jake nodded. "We might have to compromise or risk losing the only girl I ever gave a damn about." He looked at Tucker. "You know we have to."

"No, we don't."

Jake tipped his head toward Molly.

Dusty dipped her into a deep pose and pulled her back up into his arms.

Her cheeks were flushed and her smile wouldn't stop.

"Fuck," Tucker said. "We have to talk about this. Let's go."

"THEY'RE GONE," Molly stopped dancing, laughing and smiling as soon as the Maddox brothers left the saloon. "Thank you, Dusty. I hope we taught those boys a lesson."

"Yeah." Dusty didn't release her right away, his lips twisting. "You know, if things don't work out for you with Tucker and Jake, I'm available Tuesday and

Wednesday nights." He smiled down at her. "I want to take you out."

Molly patted Dusty's cheek. "Oh, sweetie, I'd love to, but I couldn't go with you in clear conscience when I'm wrapped up, crazy for Jake and Tucker."

"Why don't you just pick one of them?"

She sighed. "I like them both. Tucker is big, stoic and incredibly passionate beneath his gruff exterior. And Jake..." She laughed. "He's full of surprises and keeps things interesting. Having both of them would be the best of both worlds."

"What if they choose not to go along with your demands?" Dusty stared at the door the Maddox men had left through. "Most men aren't into sharing their woman. Not even with their brother."

"That's what's so great about where we live. Look around." She waved toward the saloon. "Three of my brothers love one woman, and she loves all three of them. Mark and Luke love Libby. Jack Monahan and Cory McBride both love Bunny, and she loves them." Molly gripped Dusty's arm. "It can work. I know it can." She bit her lip. "Can't it?"

Dusty tipped his head. "Maybe. Thing is, Jake and Tucker have been competing against each other all their lives. Anything Tucker does, Jake has to try and do better. They were that way in sports and in flying. Fortunately, they need both a helicopter *and* a fixed-wing pilot or they'd be flying circles around each other, playing chicken in the sky."

Molly knew that. She'd known them her whole life and had fallen in love with them way before they'd finally asked her out. "Do you think I'm making a mistake? I don't want to lose them."

"If you make them choose between sharing you and losing you, don't be surprised if they take the easier route."

"Losing me?" Molly's chest squeezed hard. "I don't want to lose them. But I can't choose. If I pick Tucker, I'll always wonder how it would have been with Jake. And vice versa. Besides, how would the man I didn't choose handle seeing me with his brother? It could tear them apart." She shook her head. "No, it's all or nothing. That's the only way it *can* be."

"Your choice, Molly." Dusty stared down at her. "Remember, you owe me."

"I'll be there tomorrow, wearing a dress and lipstick. I promise."

He lifted her hand to his lips. "You're a life-saver."

"It's the least I can do. You helped me in a pinch. I can help you."

He lifted her hand to his lips and pressed a kiss to her knuckles. "Again, if it all falls through, I'm here for you." He winked and twirled her away from him and back into his arms. "Thanks for the dance." He left her standing on the edge of the dance floor and walked out of the saloon.

"Dusty's a nice guy." Audrey stopped next to her, resting a hand on her belly. "You could do worse."

"Yeah, but I'm not in love with Dusty."

"I know. You're in love with the Maddox men." Audrey patted her back. "Things have a way of working out."

"I hope you're right." Molly got back to work waiting tables and filling orders. If she was wrong, she'd just have to pull up stakes and head to Austin like she'd threatened her brothers she would.

Austin was looking more and more depressing by the minute.

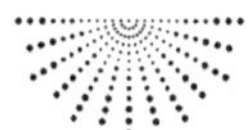

CHAPTER SIX

Jake arrived at the Maddox Air Charter Service offices earlier than Tucker the following day. They'd agreed on the way home the previous night not to talk about the situation with Molly until they'd had time to sleep on it.

Sleep hadn't come easy to Jake. He'd gone to bed thinking *to hell with her.* When he woke, he knew he couldn't just let go and move on. Molly was everything he could ever want in a forever mate. Though he'd played the field since he was a teen, he knew once he found the right girl he'd settle down and devote the rest of his life to making her happy.

Molly was the girl. If sharing her with another man made her happy, who was he to balk? He and Tucker could work out a schedule. One of them could be with her one night, and switch out with the other the next night. They didn't have to get naked with her at the same time.

It could work.

The more Jake thought about it, the more convinced he became that Molly could have them both and they could be as happy sharing her.

The one fly in the ointment was Tucker. His brother liked things the way he liked things, neat orderly and normal. A ménage to Tucker was *not* normal. He'd be uptight and possibly willing to give up on Molly if she stuck to her guns and insisted on both of them loving her, not just one.

On the one hand, if Tucker backed out, it would leave Molly free to be with Jake. His heartbeat fluttered. Having her all to himself would be heaven.

Pulse slowing, Jake realized it wouldn't work. Molly had been crystal clear about both of them or neither. If Tucker backed out, that ruined things for Jake as well.

He had a tough task ahead of him. Convincing Tucker he should share Molly with him might require some major finagling.

The sound of a plane pulling up outside on the tarmac signaled Tuck's arrival. Jake stepped out of the office to greet him.

Tucker stepped down from the plane and extended a hand to the couple getting out behind him.

Jake opened the storage bin, pulled out their suitcases and set them on the tarmac. "Did you have a nice flight?" he asked politely.

The woman, in her fifties, slim and still beautiful, smiled. "It was lovely and the landing was so smooth." She patted Tucker's cheek. "Thank you, son. We'll definitely recommend your service to our friends."

Her husband stuck out a hand and shook Tucker's then Jake's. "Top notch. Top notch," was all he said.

Tucker and Jake carried their luggage to the Lincoln Town Car they'd parked outside the office. After stowing their luggage and waving goodbye, Jake followed Tucker into the office.

The second the door closed behind Jake, Tucker spun to face him. "Look, I'm not willing to lose Molly."

"Me either," Jake agreed.

"So what are we going to do about it?"

"Cave in to her wishes?" Jake offered.

Tucker paced the length of his office. He stopped, dragged a hand down his face and turned to Jake. "Yeah. We give her what she wants." He looked at his brother. "I'm not sure how this will work, and I'm not totally comfortable sharing a woman with you, but damn it!" He pounded a fist on the surface of his desk. "Molly's worth it!"

Jake grinned. "I had the same thought. If either of us backs out, it's over with Molly."

"I'm not willing to let that happen." Tucker's eyes narrowed. "So don't even think about backing out."

Jake raised his hands. "Me? *You* were the one I was sure would say hell no."

Tucker nodded toward the door. "Let's get this place locked down. We have a woman to go see."

"Yes, we do." Jake followed Tucker. "The sooner the better."

Tucker came to a halt so fast, Jake ran into him. "Oh, hell."

"What?" Jake asked.

Tucker cursed again. "I forgot."

"Forgot what?"

"We have that damned garden club benefit for the women's shelter tonight. We promised Sandell and Rutherford we'd be there."

Jake pushed past Tucker. "Those old busybodies won't notice if we're not there."

"No. But we promised," Tucker insisted.

Jake cringed. Nothing he could say would sway his brother. Tucker stood by his promises, even when made to the president and vice president of the Temptation Garden Club.

"Look," Tucker said. "All we have to do is make a showing. Then we can leave."

Jake turned back to Tucker, grinning. "Maybe we can take Molly on our first date as a threesome."

Tucker's face brightened. "That's a great idea. I bet she's going anyway. It would show our unity by asking her to go with us."

Jake pulled out his cell phone and dialed Molly's

number, and then hit the speaker button so that Tucker could be in on the conversation as well.

"Sean speaking," a deep, male voice answered.

"This is Jake," Jake turned to his brother.

Tucker stared at him and then added quickly, "and Tucker Maddox."

"What can I do for ya?"

"Is Molly there?" Jake asked.

Sean paused and a muffled yell came across, "Is Molly here?"

A moment later, Sean came back on the line. "Nope. She's out on a date with Dusty Cramer."

Jake stared at Tucker, a lead weight settling in the pit of his belly.

Tucker leaned over the phone. "Thanks, Sean. Could you tell her we called?"

"Sure, but aren't you going to the benefit tonight? You can tell her yourself. That's where she and Dusty went."

"Thanks we will." Tucker hit the END button and stared across at Jake. "We have to do some damage control. Molly might have changed her mind."

Jake's gut clenched. "After the ruckus we raised last night, she might not want either one of us."

"Damn."

"Well, let's get going." Jake clapped a hand to Tucker's back. "We have a benefit to attend."

"God, I hate these garden party fundraisers with

tea and finger food," Tucker muttered. "I'd skip it if I hadn't already committed."

"We can't skip, now," Jake said. "Dusty's moving in on our girl."

Tucker's jaw tightened. "And we're not about to lose her to someone else."

"No." Tucker headed for the plane. "We're not." He secured the tie-down straps and checked over the craft in preparation for the next day's sortie.

Jake double-checked the helicopter. When all was locked up and secured for the night, the two men drove home.

"Tonight's event is formal," Jake said as he hurried up the steps of the front porch.

"I'm wearing my jeans." Tucker headed for his room while Jake entered his.

"The hell you are," Jake called out. "Wear your suit."

"Fuck. I hate suits."

"You might hate them, but women love them on a man." Jake pulled his one and only suit out of the closet and shook off the dust. The last time he'd worn it had been to his uncle's funeral. Well tonight he'd wear it for another good cause. Winning Molly back from Dusty Cramer. Damned claim jumper.

MOLLY WALKED into Mrs. Rutherford's garden on

Dusty Cramer's arm, wearing a dress, high heels and lipstick—three things she hated most. They ranked right up there with hairspray and tiaras. Not Molly's style. Oh, she didn't mind dresses as long as she could go barefoot or wear her cowboy boots with them. But mostly, she didn't like getting all dressed up to attend a stuffy social function.

But the cause was good. The money raised with the silent auction would benefit the women's shelter, which, along with the rest of the town was slowly recovering from a twister that had touched down over a year ago. She couldn't complain too much since she was helping out Dusty, whose elderly mother was also a member of the Temptation Garden Club, by showing up as his date.

Molly glanced up at Dusty. "Why didn't you bring a *real* date?"

"I would if I could find one. In case you haven't noticed, a lot of the women in Temptation are taken. And I'm picky. I don't want to date someone just for this event. It wouldn't be fair to the young lady when I don't call her ever again."

"Why is it so important to show up at the fundraiser with a date?"

"I hope by bringing you, my mother will get off my back about getting married and having children." He nodded toward a woman sitting at a bistro table on the back patio. "See that woman?"

Molly nodded. "Mrs. Rheinhardt."

"She's the problem."

"How so?" Molly knew the woman. She was nice enough and had a huge family that lived in and around Temptation.

"She constantly brags about her daughters and all her grandchildren. She has half the mamas in the county badgering their sons and daughters to get married and produce."

"Oh." Molly smiled and waved at Mrs. Rheinhardt. "I see your problem. But won't your mother be disappointed when I don't show up with you at any other event?"

"She'll get over it. At least for tonight she won't give me hell." He pulled Molly's arm through his. "Now put on your happy face. Here comes my mother."

Molly pasted a smile on her face and greeted Mrs. Cramer.

"Molly, darlin'," Mrs. Cramer exclaimed. "So happy to see you. Why, I remember when you were a little bitty thing, following your big brothers around at the Fourth of July Barbeques. Your mother and I used to be such friends, bless her soul." She pulled Molly into a hug and squished the air from her lungs.

When she finally let go, Molly felt awful. Not from the bear hug, but from lying to one of her mother's old friends. "Nice to see you again, Mrs. Cramer."

Mrs. Cramer turned to Mrs. Rheinhardt, urging Molly forward. "Winnie, honey, look who Dusty brought with him this evening. Why, it's Molly O'Brien."

Mrs. Rheinhardt squinted up at Molly. "Oh, yes. The youngest of the O'Brien clan, God bless her mother's soul. When is your father coming back from Australia?"

Like Molly had told her brothers, everybody knew everything about everyone. "He'll be back in a month or so."

The older woman glanced from Molly to Dusty and back. "Is this something new? Are you two a couple?"

Mrs. Cramer laughed. "Oh, Winnie, don't rush the young folks. I'm sure they'll make up their minds soon enough."

Molly was herded away, dragging Dusty with her. She'd be damned if she let him off the hook with his mother making a show of the woman her son brought to the big event.

She was on display with Mrs. Rutherford and Mrs. Sandell, the president and vice president of the Temptation Garden club, when Jake and Tucker arrived. Molly didn't have to turn around to know they were behind her. She could feel every nerve ending come alive, and her core tightened.

Schooling her face to calm, she turned slowly as though she were admiring the roses in Mrs. Rutherford's garden, her gaze connecting with Tucker's and then Jake's.

Their smoldering blue gazes captured and held hers so long she felt a little lightheaded and didn't hear Mrs. Rutherford's question.

"I'm sorry," Molly turned back to the older woman. "What was it you were saying?"

"I asked when you're going to marry and settle down," Mrs. Rutherford frowned. "Are you all right, dear? Your face is flushed."

"You should have a seat." Mrs. Sandell led her to a chair by a wrought iron bistro table and pushed her into it. "I'll get you a glass of cool lemonade."

"No, really, I'm fine." And she'd much rather have a beer. Whiskey would be even better. A glass of lemonade was slapped into her hand, and she forced herself to smile, thank Mrs. Sandell and then sip the tart lemon-flavored water until her mouth puckered.

Mrs. Rheinhardt leaned close to Mrs. Sandell. "You know, my body ran hot when I was in the family way."

Molly was in mid-sip when she overheard the older woman whispering to her friend. She choked on the liquid and spewed it out, all over Mrs. Rutherford's prize grandiflora roses.

"Oh, dear!" Mrs. Rutherford raced forward and stood between her roses and Molly. "If you're going to be ill, please, feel free to use the bathroom in my house. But above all, spare the roses!"

Molly lurched to her feet, teetered on her heels and grabbed for Dusty's arm. "Get me out of here," she whispered into his ear. "Now."

"If you'll excuse us, I'll help Molly into the house." Dusty guided her into the Rutherford home.

Once inside the air-conditioned entrance, Molly turned on Dusty. "I am not in a family way and I don't like lying to those old women. Before you know it, they'll have me married off and pregnant with triplets."

Dusty laughed. "You can't let them get to you. But now you see what I've been dealing with. My mother and the ladies of the Temptation Garden Club have nothing better to do than gossip."

"Well, I don't like being the source of their gossip." Molly stepped away from Dusty. "I'm going to splash water on my face, and then I'll be ready to leave. Go out and mingle until then. I can't face them." She snorted. "Pregnant. Me! Ha!"

Dusty left her to find the bathroom on her own.

After splashing water on her heated cheeks, careful not to smear her mascara, she patted her face dry and stared at her reflection.

Pregnant.

Molly ran her hands over her flat belly, thinking of how happy Audrey was carrying Jackson's child.

Sure, Molly had thoughts of being pregnant some day. She could picture a dark-haired, blue-eyed little boy running around the yard, or a pretty green-eyed girl riding bareback across the pasture, her hair flying out behind her. Yeah, she'd like to get married and have kids, but she had to have a husband first.

Jake and Tucker flashed through her mind. Maybe she was wrong asking them to share her. No matter how hard she tried, she couldn't pick one over the other. Austin was looking like the only alternative that would work. Her family was not going to like it, and frankly, she'd miss her father, brothers, Audrey, Jackson and all the people she knew and loved.

Temptation was a small community and the people were pretty close. In Austin, she'd be a little fish in a big pond, out of her element and lost in the crowd. Then again, she'd be away from the gossips and busybodies.

With a sigh, she stepped out of the powder room and ran into a solid wall of muscle.

Molly squeaked and backed up so fast she tripped over her damned high heels.

Hands reached out, grabbed her and slammed her into those muscles again, holding her tightly. "Hey, darlin'."

Her knees melted and she looked up into Tucker Maddox's blue eyes. "You have a way of knocking a girl off her feet."

His chuckle rumbled against her chest, vibrating her breasts where they smashed against him. "I'm a man with technique."

Warmth stole into her cheeks and her fingers

curled into his shirt. Yeah, he had technique. When his tongue flicked her... Molly stopped right there. She couldn't think about Tucker and the way he made her crazy. Not when she was there as another man's date.

She pulled back, straightened her dress and shoulders. "Tucker, I'm surprised to see you and your brother here. A garden party doesn't strike me as your kind of thing."

"I'm all for a good cause." His brows puckered. "Look, Molly. Dusty isn't the guy for you."

Molly's brows furrowed. "And you know this because?"

"He's just not."

"And you are?" She pushed past him. "I'm sorry, but I'm with Dusty tonight. Not you and your brother. I'd appreciate it if you didn't interfere." Though she wanted to fall into his arms and beg him to take her away from the frumpy women with their gossiping tongues, Molly left the house and headed straight for Dusty, a smile pasted to her face. "I think I'm not feeling quite well." Let the biddies make what they would of that. "Could you take me home?"

Dusty's concerned frown made Molly feel guilty, but she couldn't stay with Dusty when she wanted to be with Tucker and Jake. It was best if she left. If the Maddox brothers wanted her, they'd have to come to her on her terms. But not until her date with Dusty was over.

She passed Tucker and Jake on her way out, keeping her head down, refusing to make eye contact with them.

As she cleared the gate, she removed her heels and ran to Dusty's truck as fast as she could in the thigh-constricting dress. She couldn't play the games required of her. For one, Dusty deserved a woman who loved him. Secondly, Molly wanted two men but would be forced to leave them both to keep the peace.

Her life sucked.

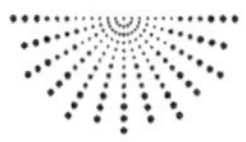

CHAPTER SEVEN

Jake backhanded Tucker in the gut. "What did you say to her?"

"I don't know." Tucker ran a hand through his hair. "All I told her was that Dusty wasn't right for her."

"Did you tell her that we'd agreed to share her like she wanted?"

"She didn't give me a chance. She said she was with Dusty and not to interfere."

"Fuck." Jake clapped a hand over his mouth when he noted Mrs. Rutherford glaring at him. He gave her a weak smile. "I mean fudge."

Her frown lightened, and she turned back to her conversation with Mrs. Sandell.

Jake grabbed Tucker's arm and led him through the garden gate to the street.

"We can't leave," Tucker protested. "We just got here."

"We're leaving. I don't give a rat's ass what those old ladies think. Molly gave you the brush off. We've reached a critical point in our relationship with her. We have to do something fast or risk losing her forever."

Tucker paced out into the street and back to the curb. "What do you suggest?"

"We have to do something drastic. Something that proves to her we're serious."

"We have to get her away from Dusty," Tucker stated, his tone flat.

"That, too." Jake took his turn pacing out into the street. A crazy, absolutely insane idea popped into his head, and he stopped in the middle of the street. He stared across at Tucker.

"Uh oh. I've seen that look before." Tucker held up his hands. "It almost got us thrown in jail when we were teens."

The idea blossomed and a grin spread across his face. "I know what we have to do."

"Yeah, I'm afraid to ask what." Tucker shook his head. "Whatever your idea is, my answer is no."

Jake frowned. "You haven't even heard it yet."

Tucker stood tall, his shoulders back, his chin high. "The answer is still no."

Jake grabbed his brother's arm. "Come on, we

can't let anyone hear what it is. If we want this to work, we have to keep it secret."

Tucker resisted all the way to Jake's truck, but climbed into the passenger seat. "So what's the big idea? Not that I'm agreeing to it."

Before he revealed his epiphany, Jake shifted into drive and pulled away from Mrs. Rutherford's house and onto the road to home.

He drove to the edge of town before he shot a glance toward Tucker. "We're going to kidnap Molly and take her away to our hunting cabin in West Texas."

Tucker burst out laughing. "That's what you've got? Kidnapping?" He held his side. "Please, you're hurting my bruised rib."

"It's the only way we can get her away from all other distractions and show her that we can get along and share her the way she wants."

Tucker continued to chuckle, though the sound faded as time passed.

Jake glared at his brother. "You got any better ideas?"

His brother's laughter stopped completely. "No."

"Did you like seeing her with Dusty? I heard the old ladies were speculating about her being pregnant before they're even married."

A ruddy red flush crept into Tucker's cheeks and his jaw tightened. "I like Dusty, but he's not the right man for Molly."

"Damn right, he's not." Jake slapped his own chest. "*We* are."

"Yes, we are." Tucker sat forward, his eyes narrowing. "How do you propose we grab her?"

Jake's pulse leaped. "She rides her horse every afternoon before she goes to work at the Ugly Stick." Jake's foot pressed hard on the accelerator and they flew toward the ranch. "We can take her then. What do you have on the books tomorrow?"

"A morning flight to Austin," Tucker said. "I'll be back by noon. The rest of the weekend is free." Tucker glanced at Jake. "What about you?"

"My booking cancelled. I'm free until Monday."

"Perfect." Tucker nodded. "While I'm gone, you can gather what we'll need for two days in West Texas. Food, water, clean sheets for the beds, the usual stuff we take when we go hunting, minus guns."

"And plenty of condoms and lubricant." Jake grinned. "We'll have to take the helicopter to get in, grab Molly and get out."

"I could land the plane in one of their pastures."

Jake shook his head. "We can't risk snagging a fence." His hands tightened on the steering wheel, his mind made up.

His brother nodded. "The helicopter it is."

Jake stuck out a hand. Tucker took it and they shook. "Tomorrow."

～

AFTER DUSTY DROPPED MOLLY OFF at the ranch, she spent the night pacing her bedroom floor, wishing she could pick up the phone and call Jake and Tucker. But what would she say—*I want you. Please choose to be with me?* It wasn't in her nature to beg, and now wasn't the time to start.

The Maddox men had to decide for themselves whether or not they could live with her ultimatum. In the meantime, she might as well get her affairs in order for a move to Austin. She figured the chances were slim the men would agree to her conditions.

The next morning, Molly started by cleaning out her closet, sorting through clothes she'd had since high school. She packed those away in a box for the women's shelter, along with shoes, cowboy boots and the collection of stuffed animals she'd crammed onto a back shelf.

Her brothers had Isabella. Her father wouldn't be home for another month and Jesse lived in NYC. It was time for Molly to move out of her home. She was a grown woman and needed to establish a life of her own.

Molly carried several boxes out to her car and ran them into town before she could change her mind. There were people who needed those things more than she needed to hang on to her past.

By the early afternoon, she'd had her share of dust and cobwebs. She needed the open spaces and fresh air she could only get by taking her horse out for a ride. Out in the barn, she mucked stalls, fed and watered the animals. Her brothers and Isabella had gone to Dallas for a horse auction and wouldn't be back until late that night.

She had the place to herself. Normally, she loved the peace and quiet, but today, she'd never felt more alone. As she saddled Little Joe, her eyes burned with unshed tears. When she moved to Austin, she wouldn't be able to ride every day. Her gelding would get lazy, and she'd miss him terribly.

Molly straightened her shoulders. "It's for the best. I can't live in the past. I can't ask people to do things that aren't in their nature. I have to move on."

With her mind made up, she rode out across the pasture, letting her horse have his head, racing over the hills and straight to the valley the creek ran through.

Little Joe had a kind of homing beacon. He headed there every time.

Molly couldn't deny him. She'd pushed Little Joe hard, and he probably needed a drink.

When the horse trotted to a halt, Molly sat for a moment, staring at the pool where she'd made love to Jake.

Those tears that had been threatening spilled over and fell down her cheeks. She dropped down out of her saddle and stood, staring at the creek.

Little Joe left her standing where she landed and walked to the edge of the water for a drink.

"Oh, Little Joe," Molly said, her voice cracking. "I can't leave. I love this place. I love you, and I love Jake and Tucker. It will kill me to leave everything behind."

Molly never cried. With four older brothers, she didn't dare, lest they call her a sissy. But alone on the ranch, with nobody to tease her and a sympathetic horse to console her, Molly couldn't hold back the tears. She cried, softly at first. The more she thought about leaving the deeper her sorrow.

When she couldn't cry anymore, she shucked her clothes and boots and dove into the water, letting it soothe her ravaged face and wrap around her like a caress. She swam back and forth across the pool, hoping to wear herself out, hoping that when she got back to the house, she'd fall into bed and sleep until her heart healed.

With her head in the water, all she could hear was the sound of her breathing. She was alone.

~

"THERE!" Jake pointed to a line of trees snaking through a valley. "That's the creek where Molly and I made love."

Tucker leaned forward, his heart in his throat, his pulse banging against his eardrums. He ignored the stab of jealousy that zinged through him at Jake's words. He'd have to get used to sharing Molly, much as he didn't want to. Hell, he'd rather share her than lose her.

It wasn't lost on him that what they were about to do was illegal, if the woman wasn't a willing participant. "You realize we could go to jail for this."

"Only if she presses charges," Jake responded, his voice crackling in the headset.

An animal detached itself from the trees, moving slowing, grazing in the grass. Tucker squinted. It had a saddle. "There's her horse."

"What did I tell you?" Jake grinned. "She's right on schedule."

"Molly is a creature of habit." Tucker liked that about her along with a dozen other things he could name easily. "Unless that's her brother's horse." How would they explain themselves if they ran into one of the O'Brien men? "Maybe we should reconsider."

"The hell we are." Jake maneuvered the yoke, sending the helicopter toward the earth. "I'm putting down."

The closer they got the more Tucker realized it was too late to back out. He steeled his resolve and prepared to capture the woman of their dreams and whisk her away.

Jake set down the bird and shut down the engines. They'd talked about Jake staying with the craft and Tucker going after their prize, but nixed that idea. If Molly put up resistance, one man might not be enough to haul her from the creek into the helicopter without someone getting hurt. Jake and Tucker agreed. No one was to get hurt on this mission.

Jake pulled his headset off and set it aside. "Ready?"

"As ready as I'll ever be," Tucker said. "Let's do this." He dropped to the ground and hurried toward the creek, Jake jogging to keep up.

As he neared the creek, Tucker heard the sound of splashing water. Passing through the brush, he emerged onto a solid rock ledge overlooking a clear pool with a beautiful, naked woman floating on her back, her dark hair fanning around her shoulders. "Wow," Tucker whispered.

"I know. That was what I thought when I first saw her here." Jake pulled his T-shirt over his head and tossed it to the ground.

Tucker frowned. "What are you doing?"

Jake looked at him like he was a little dense. "I'm going in after her. We can't grab her just standing here." He shucked his boots and jeans in record time and dove into the water.

Not to be left out, Tucker followed suit, stripped and jumped in.

Jake reached her first.

Molly, startled by the intrusion, lost her rhythm, sank beneath the surface and came up coughing. "Jake! What the hell?"

Jake's arms surrounded her and lifted her head

above the water. "Come here." He swam her toward the shore, stopping when he was waist-deep.

Molly got her feet under her and stood, the tips of her bare breasts bobbing on the surface. "You really have to stop sneaking up on me."

Jake grinned. "We've reached a decision."

Pushing her wet hair out of her face, Molly snorted. "And you had to come out here and scare the beejeezus out of me to tell me? You could have called or sent me a text."

Tucker swam up to her other side and slipped his arm around her. "We couldn't wait. And what we had to say needed to be delivered in person."

Molly frowned, her eyes red-rimmed, puffy and suspiciously shiny. "Well, I'm not sure I'm ready to hear what you have to say. I need a little more time to prepare."

"Darlin', we're here and the time is now." Jake's mouth quirked on the corners. He stared across at Tucker. "Ready?"

Molly's gaze narrowed and she looked from Jake to Tucker and back to Jake. "Ready for what?"

"For Operation Molly," Jake said.

Tucker nodded. "Let's do this." He bent and tossed Molly over his shoulder in a fireman's carry and plowed through the water to the shore. "Get our clothes!"

"Put me down!" Molly demanded.

She pounded his back with her fists, the blows

not nearly as hard as they could have been, giving Tucker hope she still cared about him. They'd have a lot of explaining to do. But that would have to wait until they were in the air and on the way to West Texas.

Barefooted, he charged up the creek bank and out into the pasture where the helicopter waited.

Jake jogged up beside him, wearing his boots and jeans and carrying a handful of clothes and boots. He passed Tucker, tossed what he had into the back and settled into the pilot's seat.

Tucker dumped Molly on the backseat and climbed in on top of her. The engine hummed to life and the blades started rotating. They'd planned for Jake to fly. Tucker was to keep their hostage from jumping out before they left the ground.

"What are you doing?" Molly pressed her hands against his chest and shoved as hard as she could.

With Molly's naked body rubbing against Tucker's, his cock twitched and rocketed to attention. But she was wiggling to get free and nearly kneed him in the balls.

"Damn it, woman. Be still!" Tucker wrapped his arms around hers and wound his legs around her to keep her from kicking him. "Go!" he shouted to Jake.

The helicopter lifted off the ground and rose into the air.

Tucker remained on top of Molly until they were well above five hundred feet above the earth. Then he eased up, reached behind him and closed the door.

Molly sat up and pushed away from him, staring out the opposite window as they ascended and headed west. "What the hell are you doing?" She snatched at the clothing on the floor and rifled through. "You didn't even get my clothes! What if this hunk of junk crashes? They'll find our bodies naked. Holy shit! I'm being kidnapped!"

Tucker didn't like the crazed look in Molly's eyes or the way her voice rose with each word. "We're not going to crash. Jake is the best helicopter pilot around, next to me. We know what we're doing."

"Seriously?" Molly crossed her arms over her chest and stared at Tucker like he'd grown horns. "You two know what you're doing?" She grabbed for Jake's white T-shirt with the Budweiser logo and pulled it over her head and down her torso. It was long enough to cover even her private parts, much to Tucker's disappointment. Then she poked a finger at his chest. "Take me back to the Rocking O. Now."

Tucker shook his head and reached for his head-set. "Can't until tomorrow night."

Her lips thinned and she dragged in a deep breath, letting it out slowly. "You can. And. You will."

Settling his headset over his ears, he plugged into the wall mount. "She's mad and wants to go home."

"You know the answer," Jake reminded him.

Tucker gave her a thin smile. "Sorry, you're going

for a ride with us. You might as well get comfortable. It'll be at least forty-five minutes before we get there."

"This is ridiculous." Flags of color flew in Molly's cheeks. "Just where is *there*?"

"West Texas," Tucker responded. "Our hunting cabin."

"I have to work tonight." Her eyes rounded. "And what will my brothers think when they get home to my horse wandering around with its saddle on and no sign of me? They'll go ape-shit nuts and call out the police, the sheriff and the National Guard. You two are going to be in so much trouble."

"I left a note with Audrey saying you'd be gone for the weekend, and I texted your brothers letting them know you would be with us and not to worry. Jackson Gray Wolf is on his way now to take care of your horse and the clothes we left behind." Tucker was pretty proud they'd thought to take care of all the loose ends before launching this insane operation.

Now all they had to do was calm Molly enough to show her how much they cared about her, and that the three of them could make it work.

The only thing they hadn't taken into consideration was how mad Molly would be over the kidnapping.

Tucker hoped she'd get over it soon. They had great plans, which included lubricating oils and edible underwear.

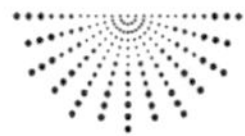

CHAPTER EIGHT

Molly maintained her angry countenance even though she was secretly thrilled by all the trouble the men had gone to in order to steal her away for a weekend. She couldn't let them know just how sexy and erotic it was to be tossed naked into the back of Jake's helicopter by the equally naked and incredibly muscled Tucker.

She was disappointed when he slipped into his jeans, shirt and boots, covering all that lovely tanned skin. Her pussy creamed, and she squirmed on the seat. Just how far were they taking her? She hoped they'd get there soon and that the bed would be big enough for the three of them.

Holly hell. Her insides burned with desire. She couldn't wait for Jake and Tucker to show her just how they were going to convince her a threesome between them would work.

She fully expected the two men to squabble and argue over her. Molly couldn't live with that. If they couldn't come together amicably, she refused to be the woman who came between the brothers. It had to work. With hope blossoming in her chest, she fought to tamp it down. But it was hard when she was with the two men she loved, and they were willing to give her demands a try.

Still, Molly didn't want to make it too easy on them. After all, they had kidnapped her.

The terrain below grew steadily more arid the farther west they flew. Finally, Jake slowed the craft and hovered over a small cabin in the middle of what looked like a desert. A dirt road led in from a paved highway a mile or two away. Wow, this was out in the back of beyond, even for a ranch girl like Molly. A thrill of excitement and trepidation trickled down the back of her neck as she pressed her nose to the window.

The cabin was a wooden structure, the boards graying. Whatever paint or stain had been applied had long since faded. It could have been an abandoned building for all she knew. Not her idea of a haven of lust. "This is it?" she commented. "You're going to convince me to give you two a shot in a derelict building held together by rusty nails?"

Tucker pulled off his headset and chuckled. "Doesn't look like much, but it'll do."

Jake tucked his headset into a flight bag. "It's better on the inside. When we're hunting we don't particularly care about our sleeping arrangements as long as we're dry and can heat a cup of coffee."

Molly snorted. "Great. We're sleeping on the floor with the scorpions."

"No," Tucker said. "There are two full-sized beds with real mattresses. We're not *that* primitive."

Jake climbed down from the helicopter and circled to the opposite side, opening the door for her.

Scooting her bare bottom to the edge, she leaned out. "Could I at least call my brothers and let them know I'm all right?"

Jake caught her around the middle and set her on the ground. "Sorry. No cell service for at least fifty miles around."

She waved toward the helicopter. "Can't you patch me in with your radio?"

Tucker shook his head. "The radio is for emergency purposes only. I don't recommend it."

"I have no clothes, no shoes and have been kidnapped by two insane criminals. You don't think that's an emergency?"

"We'll take you home tomorrow," Tucker said. "We promise."

"What if I don't want to be here?" She crossed her arms. "Isn't what you're doing wrongful imprisonment, or something like that? Are you going to do unspeakable things to me?" Her pussy clenched.

Jake's eyes widened. "No. We won't do anything you don't want us to do. What do you take us for?"

"We're not animals." Tucker glanced across at Jake. "I told you this was a bad idea."

Jake glared. "We're in it now. Don't go getting soft on me."

Molly almost laughed at the worry in Tucker's expression and the determination in Jake's. She almost broke down and told them that she was okay with their so-called operation. Her insides fairly vibrated with excitement at the thought of what they had planned next. Hopefully, it was something to do with sex.

Molly took one step toward the cabin but got no farther before Tucker scooped her into his arms and carried her to the door. Jake beat him there and inserted a key into what appeared to be a fairly modern lock. He pushed the door open and stood back for Tucker to carry Molly through.

Surprisingly, it was clean, dust-free and smelled fresh, not at all what Molly would have expected from its outward appearance.

Jake glanced around. "I had Rosa come out and give the cabin a good cleaning and airing this morning."

Tucker set Molly on the ground and nodded. "Good thinking."

"Okay, so it's not a pigsty. What now?" Molly stood in Jake's T-shirt, nipples hardened into beads making little points on the fabric. While she held back and continued to give the appearance of being angry, she was counting the minutes until they got down to what she looked forward to...S.E.X.

"I'll get the supplies." Tucker left the cabin.

Molly wandered around the one-room building that served as bedroom and kitchen all in one. Two full-sized beds were pushed up against the far side of the room with two feet of space between them and at the foot. A quick shove and the two beds could work as one big enough for three.

Her heart pounded and her belly tightened.

"Are you really mad at us?" Jake came up behind her and gripped her hips in his big hands, turning her to face him. "If you want us to take you back, we will."

Seeing Jake, the womanizer and wilder one of the pair, so very serious and offering to take her home melted Molly's resolve to hold back and make the men work for it. She raised her hands to his chest and stared up into blue eyes she could so easily fall into. Eyes the same color as his brother's. "No. You two went to a lot of trouble. I'm interested to see if being with the two of you will work."

Tucker entered the open door, carrying a large cardboard box. "Good, because I'd hate to see Jake go to jail for cooking up this crazy idea." He set it on the table and stared at Molly and Jake. "If you're going to kiss and make up, do it. I'll wait my turn."

Molly laughed and glanced up from beneath her lashes as Jake. "Well?"

"You don't have to tell me twice." His arms went around her and tightened as he bent to capture her lips, his tongue slipping past her teeth to tangle with hers.

All thoughts of leaving the cabin and going back to the Rocking O flew from Molly's mind. The kiss was so hot. Her thigh automatically climbed up Jake's, and she rubbed her pussy against his thickly muscled leg.

Tucker cleared his throat behind her. "I'd like to get in on some of that action."

Jake slowly released her, his eyes glazed with passion. He stepped back and nodded at his brother.

Molly didn't have time to turn. Tucker's hands came from behind, skimmed across her waist and pulled her back to his front.

The hard evidence of his desire pressed against her buttocks. She leaned her head to the side, giving him access to the slope of her neck. He moved his hands to her breasts. He cupped both of them, tweaking her nipples between his thumbs and fore-fingers.

"Wow," Jake said, adjusting his jeans. "I'm hot just watching."

"Tucker can't get to *all* my erogenous zones,"

Molly prompted, lifting her T-shirt, exposing the thatch of hair at the apex of her thighs. "In case I haven't made myself clear, I'm on fire and I want both of you."

Jake's eyes flared and he moved closer, brushing his fingers across her belly to weave into the curls over her sex. He parted her folds, stroked her clit and slipped down to her entrance. "Oh, babe, you are so wet."

Tucker moaned and nipped her neck, pressing the hard ridge of his fly into her bottom. He had entirely too many clothes on, and Molly was quickly becoming impatient to get to the good stuff. She reached behind her and flicked the button open on his jeans.

When she reached for the zipper, he dropped his hands to cover hers and took over, easing the zipper down, careful not to snag himself in the teeth.

Molly wrapped her hand around his cock and spread her feet a little wider. "This could get tricky."

"We're going to make this work." Jake stepped back. "Tucker...you take her."

"I told you I want both of you. Not one at a time." Molly eyed Jake. "You're overdressed."

Jake grinned and shucked the rest of his clothes.

She turned to find Tucker toeing off his boots and dropping his jeans.

"That's more like it. Now, let's take it to the mattress." She led the way, grabbing Jake's hand as she went. Molly crawled onto the bed, having played out in her mind how things would work with multiple partners and her as the center. Jake climbed in the bed behind her and positioned himself between her legs, his hands resting on her raised ass.

Tucker stood beside the bed, frowning. "How's this supposed to work?"

She winked and crooked her finger, urging him to move closer. When Tucker's legs touched the mattress, Molly curled her fingers around his dick and lowered herself to touch her tongue to his length. She licked a circle around the rim and said, "Like this." Then she sucked his cock into her mouth.

He didn't need much encouragement. As soon as she wrapped her lips around him, he thrust into her. She took him all the way in until he bumped into the back of her throat. Holy hell, he was so big it made her cream thinking about his brother poised to enter behind her.

Jake reached beneath the pillow and pulled out a condom. "Remind me to thank Rosa." He tore it open and rolled it down over himself. Then he reached between Molly's legs, parted her folds and stroked her there until her hips swayed and her belly tightened.

One of his big fingers pressed into her channel, swirled and came out to trail a wet line of her juices up to her clit.

He touched, teased, and bent to press a kiss to

first one of her butt cheeks, then the other, his fingers never slowing in his determination to bring her to the edge.

Her breath caught in her throat as tingles ignited and spread outward. She gripped Tucker's balls and held him buried in her mouth as waves of her release washed over her.

Then Jake moved forward and thrust into her, filling her with his thickness, her channel clenching around him and drawing him deeper.

Yes. This was how she'd envisioned making love to Jake and Tucker. And it was everything she'd imagined it would be.

With her mouth full of one and her pussy full of the other, she rocked them both, shooting to the heavens along with their orgasms.

Tucker pulled out of her mouth before he lost it, his face tight as if he held on to his control by a thread.

Molly buried her face in the comforter, her fingers curling around the fabric as Jake rode her to the end.

His hands on her hips, he thrust deep into her and held her there until his cock stopped throbbing.

"Oh, sweet heaven." Molly collapsed onto the bed, rolled onto her back and spread her legs for Tucker.

Jake lay down beside her and fondled her breasts, pinching and tugging them into tight little buds.

Tucker hesitated for a moment.

Jake held up his hand. "Wait."

Tuck's jaw tightened.

His brother reached beneath the pillow again and surfaced another foil packet. He tossed it to Tucker. "Rosa is getting a huge tip."

"Damn right."

Molly watched as the older brother removed the condom from the packet and spread it down over his cock.

Protection applied, Tucker climbed between her legs.

Jake rolled to the side, giving him more room.

"Come inside me," Molly said, her voice low, her words heavy, desire rising once again to the surface.

He pressed his erection against her slick opening and paused, leaning down to capture her lips in a soul-searing kiss.

Molly wrapped her arms around his neck and her legs around his waist, and pulled him close.

Tucker slid into her, his cock filling her, the friction setting her on the path to another incredible orgasm.

"Oh, sweet, heaven. Can a person die from multiple orgasms?" she muttered.

Tucker pulled out immediately. "Are you hurting?"

She cried out. "I meant that in a good way. Please. By all that's incredible. Ride me, cowboy." Pressing her heels into his buttocks, she urged him to take her. "Fuck me hard."

"I don't want to make you sore."

"Oh, baby, it'll be the best kind of sore." Molly dug her fingernails into his back, showing him how fast she wanted it and how hard to push.

He rode her, thrusting like a piston again and again until she burst over the precipice, rocketing into space.

Tucker rammed into her one last time and collapsed, breathing hard and crushing her beneath him.

For a long moment, he lay on her and she could barely breathe, then he rolled to the side, pulling free of her.

Molly laid between them, completely satiated, her pussy throbbing, her heart full, a hand on each of her guys. This was heaven.

Then Jake opened his mouth.

"Damn, Tuck." Jake chuckled. "I didn't think you had it in you to ride a woman like a bucking bronco."

With an arm draped over his eyes, Tucker lay still, too drained to do anything but say, "Shut the fuck up."

"Just sayin'." Jake leaned up on his elbow and fondled Molly's breast, rolling the nipple between his fingers. "So, who's bigger?"

Molly frowned.

Tucker jerked to a sitting position. "That's not something you ask a lady after what we just did.

Besides, we both know the answer to that." Damn Jake for making a joke out of loving Molly.

"Yeah, you're right." Jake laughed and climbed out of the bed, his cock dangling as if to prove he was right. "We both know I'm bigger."

Tucker closed his eyes. "Next time we do it, you can take a walk outside."

"Like hell. Molly wants both of us. Not one or the other." Jake walked to the table where Tucker had left the cardboard box full of supplies. "Who's hungry?"

"Asshole," Tucker called out. "You kill the mood with your jokes."

"You're the ass." Jake pulled out a can and set it on the table.

Molly's frown and stillness alerted Tucker to trouble. He leaned up on his elbow and stared down at her. "Are you all right? Was I too rough with you?"

She shook her head and gave him a sad smile. "I can't do this."

"Do what?" Jake stopped what he was doing to look around. "Put up with Tucker?"

Tucker shot Jake a drop-dead look and returned his attention to the woman he was head over heels for. "Yeah, do what?"

"Come between you two." She crawled over Tucker and got out of the bed. Grabbing the first T-shirt she came to, she pulled it over her head and stalked out of the cabin.

Tucker glared at Jake. "See what you did?"

Jake raised his hands, palms up. "What did I do?"

Tucker didn't stop to explain. He headed out of the cabin to catch Molly before she got lost or hurt herself walking barefooted in cactus country.

"Molly wait," he called out.

"Leave me alone." She kept going, then stopped and spun around so fast he almost ran over her. "Unless you two take me home." Throwing her hand in the air, she spun and marched away again. "Never mind. You two have your cockamamie plan to make me see that you could actually share me and get along."

Tucker followed, keeping an eye open for snakes while rocks dug into the souls of his bare feet. "We're making it work, Molly. For you. We want you to be happy."

Jake caught up with them and grabbed her arm, pulling her to a stop. "Babe, we love you."

"Making me happy doesn't mean a thing if you two are miserable." Molly jerked her arm free. "I'm sorry. I can't do this to you. I love you both too much to watch your relationship as brothers fall apart."

Tucker stopped.

Jake stopped too and faced him. "What's she talking about?"

Tucker shrugged. "I haven't the slightest clue."

"Do you think our poking at each other got to her?" Jake asked.

"She might not understand that's how we are, with or without her in the picture."

"Well, hell. Are we going to just stand here in the nude with the sun beating down on us, frying our lily-white asses, or are we going to get our girl and fuck some sense into her?"

"I'm with you." Tucker stuck out his hand.

Jake took it and shook.

Tucker gave his brother a narrow-eyed glare. "That doesn't mean you can stare at my junk."

Jake laughed. "Don't worry. You're clearly not my type." He tipped his head toward the woman now a football field's length away from them and moving fast. "Now that little filly is exactly my type."

"And mine." Tucker grinned. "Let's round her up and bring her back to the barn."

Tucker led off, jogging carefully down the gravel road, cursing with each rock that dug into the tender parts of his feet.

When he and Jake caught up with Molly, they blocked her path. Tucker moved to stand in front of her.

Jake brought up the rear.

"Come back to the cabin," Tucker coaxed.

Jake turned her. "What you thought was us arguing is just the way we are with each other. Despite our bickering, we'd take a bullet for the other if we had to."

"Speak for yourself." Tucker brushed his knuckle

along the smooth line of Molly's cheek. "He's right though. We'd do anything for each other. Though I have to admit, the thought of sharing the most beautiful woman in the world never occurred to me. I have to say, watching Jake fuck you and play with you while you gave me head was...incredibly arousing."

"For me too," Jake admitted. "Seeing the way you came alive beneath Tucker while he was fucking you, only made me hotter and want you more."

Molly's brows puckered, and she bit down on her bottom lip. "Whatever happens, I don't want to come between you two."

"Darlin'." Tucker cupped her cheek. "No matter how aggravated I get with Jake, he's the only family I've got. We stick together."

"Hey, babe," Jake slipped his hand down her arm, captured her hand and lifted it to his lips. "I love that jackass. And we'll love you so much, you won't ever lack for attention."

Molly looked from Tucker to Jake. "I guess brothers will bicker. Mine do all the time." A smile pulled at the corners of her lips. "But I love my family, even if they do drive me nuts."

"Exactly." Tucker kissed her cheek. "That's how I feel about Jake and his lack of organization."

"And that's how I feel about Tucker and his annoying OCD, trying to fit me into his tiny square hole, when I'm obviously a charming, sexy, and *large* round peg." Jake gave Molly that killer smile Tucker envied.

She smiled back and leaned up on her toes to press her lips to Jake's mouth.

He swept her into his arms and deepened the kiss.

Tucker fought the urge to pry the two apart, instead he waited until Jake let go. He'd have to get used to this arrangement.

Molly immediately pressed her body against Tucker, wrapped her arms around his neck and pulled him down within kissing range.

He didn't mind seconds, because every time with Molly would be like a first. Gathering her close, he claimed her mouth.

She made the next move by thrusting her tongue past his teeth and caressing his, in a long, sensuous glide, ending with a nibble on his bottom lip.

He leaned his forehead against hers and smiled. "Welcome to the family, Molly. We're going to love you like there'll be no more tomorrows."

She kissed the tip of his nose and pulled Jake close. "I'm counting on it. Now, who's going to carry me back to bed?"

~

If you enjoyed this book, try the other books in the Ugly Stick Saloon Series

Boots & Chaps (#1)
Boots & Sex Ed (#2)
Boots & Leather (#3)
Boots & Promises (#4)
Boots & Bareback (#5)
Boots & Dirty Tricks (#6)
Boots & Lace (#7)
Boots & Roses (#8)
Boots & Buckles (#9)
Boots & the Wishes (#10)
Boots & Twisters (#11)
Boots & the Bachelor (#12)
Boots & The Rogue (#13)
Boots & The Heartbreaker (#14)
Boots & Wings (#15)

SEX, LIES & VAMPIRE HUNTERS

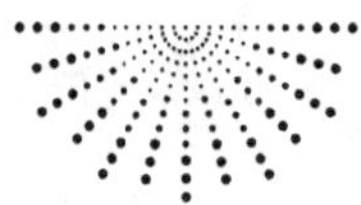

NIGHT SHIFT SERIES BOOK #1

New York Times & USA Today
Bestselling Author
ELLE JAMES

Writing as

MYLA JACKSON

Sex, Lies & Vampire Hunters
A Night Shift Novel
AWARD-WINNING AUTHOR
MYLA JACKSON

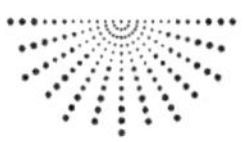

*J*ulie Taylor tipped the vial upside down and jammed the syringe into the rubber covering. Just two more hours and she could go home and get off her aching feet. When she had the desired dose, she removed the needle and set the glass vial on the cart.

"Don't look now, but guess who just pulled up in his squad car?" a gravelly, feminine voice whispered into her ear.

The bottle slipped from her suddenly nerveless fingers and would have crashed to the floor if she hadn't slammed her hip against the cart, catching it between the cart and her scrubs. Whew! "Kim Erickson, don't do that!"

Kim giggled and sashayed out of reach. "Thought you'd want to know. But if you don't care…" Her eyebrows rose questioningly. "I'll tell him you're not interested." The flirty behavior was a marked contrast to Kim's long bottle-black hair and Goth makeup. Kim was a dichotomy of sweet and weird wrapped up in a slightly plump package. Despite Kim's strange appearance, Julie couldn't find a better friend.

"Don't you dare!" Syringe in hand, Julie followed Kim out into the hallway.

"Hey! Watch it with that thing," Dorothy Lindeman, or Dottie, the battle-axe, head nurse of the nightshift, dodged around her pointed needle. "Get that medication into the patient in Room 1 before you stick someone else with it." Battle-axe in spirit only, Dorothy was anything but large and ugly. However, she could be mean when you didn't do as she said.

Julie hurried toward Room 1 where Mrs. Thompson struggled to breathe through a severe asthma attack. All the while she ministered to her patient, her thoughts were on the gorgeous cop who'd chosen to target her with his flirting ways. Damn, she was lucky. Roger Decker was the sexiest hunk this side of the Mississippi and he wanted her.

Julie sighed. If only they could get their shifts synchronized so they could spend time together.

Mrs. Thompson was resting easily, her breathing returning to normal.

Julie slipped out into the hallway and turned toward the nurses station for her next assignment.

Before she could take two steps, her friend Kim snagged her by the elbow and marched her toward the supply closet. "What? Where are you taking me?"

"Shut up. You'll thank me later." Kim opened the closet door and shoved her inside, closing the door behind her.

The closet was dark and filled with the acrid scent of disinfectant floor cleaners and old mops. Julie fumbled in the dark for the doorknob. When she found it, she twisted the handle and pulled. It didn't budge. "What's the deal?"

"I'm the deal." A low sexy voice breathed against the back of her neck.

Her muscles bunched and then relaxed when she realized who was behind her. With a sigh, she leaned back against a solid chest, inhaling the scent of musky cologne and male.

Roger. The man of her dreams. The man destined to stay in her dreams. Other than the stolen kisses in the emergency room hallway that managed to graduate into some particularly heavy groping sessions in this supply closet, she'd done little else but fantasize about this man. How she'd love to do a lot more, maybe spend an entire night together—naked.

His breath stirred the hairs that had fallen loose from the neat ponytail she'd started the night with. Arms circled around her middle, rising beneath her breasts.

"Pervert," she whispered and pressed her bottom

against the hard ridge behind his uniform trousers. While his hands slipped beneath her scrub shirt and lacy bra, she reached behind her to cup his ass. God, how she wanted him. "You're going to get me fired."

"Then we'll have time to do more of this." His tongue curled around her earlobe and he sucked it into his mouth, nibbling gently with his teeth.

"Um, perhaps I could live on sex alone?" She turned in his arms. "Who needs food or a roof over my head, when I can have all this?"

"Now you're thinking."

"Yeah, but it's time to quit thinking and start..." she pressed her lips to his, cutting off further conversation. Her time was short. She'd better make good use of it.

He pushed her bra up over her breasts and tweaked her nipples between his thumb and forefingers. Pressing his cheek against her hair, he inhaled. "You smell like heaven."

She laughed. "How can you smell anything over the disinfectant and dirty mops?"

"I can, when I'm this close." He nudged a knee between her legs, rubbing his thigh against her cunt.

When his leg touched her there, all the air whooshed out of her lungs and she clung to him.

A hand rose to cup her face in the darkness, his lips descending to claim hers in a long scorching kiss. While his tongue toyed and dueled with hers, blunt-tipped fingers slid once more beneath her shirt.

She tugged the buttons open on his uniform to comb her fingers through his chest hairs, except a cotton t-shirt stood in the way. Julie plucked at it. "You have too many clothes on." Short of pulling his shirt and t-shirt from his waistband she had to content herself with sliding her fingers between his uniform and the t-shirt. When she found the hard little knots of his nipples beneath the soft cotton, she tweaked.

The hard ridge of his cock rocked against her belly. "Your clothes are much more accessible to play." He pushed his hands beneath the elastic waistband of her scrubs and burrowed into the silky bikini underwear to the furry mound at the juncture of her thighs.

"I CAN'T BELIEVE we're doing this in a janitor's closet." Despite her words, her legs spread to give him more maneuvering room.

"I'd rather have you in my bed." With his index finger, he parted the thick folds and stroked the cleft between.

Julie moaned, her back arching, pressing her into his hand. "What if someone comes?" she gasped.

"What if you come?" He paused, his fingers cupping her sex lightly. "Do you want me to stop?"

"Are you kidding?" She grabbed his arm and pushed him deeper. "If you stop now, I'll die."

He needed no further encouragement. Like a mechanic, he dipped his finger in to test how slick and lubricated she was. "God, you're wet." He dragged creamy juices up to that sensitive nub and flicked it until Julie leaned into him, gasping. Raw need filled her, nerves jumping with every stroke, until she was spiraling up and over the edge, her pelvis jerking her release. Then she pressed her forehead to his chest. "Oh, God." With a long deep breath, she blew out in a sharp stream against his neck. "Now, your turn."

She was fumbling with his belt buckle when the door handle jerked.

"What the hell?" A male voice muttered on the other side.

Julie froze for a moment. Then her fingers dropped from his zipper. "Shit. My boss will fire me on the spot if she catches me in here with you."

"Don't sweat it, sounded more like a man than a woman out there."

"Yeah, but he might go to her for the key to the closet." She spun around in the dark, straightening her clothes, tugging her bra down over her breasts.

Roger buckled his belt and was buttoning his shirt when the door swung open.

"Kim!" Julie fell out of the closet and hugged her friend. "Thank God it's you."

"Don't thank me now, the battle-axe is on the warpath, and she's looking for you. Run the other way while I get Mr. Hot-and-Bothered out the back."

"Thanks, Kim." She turned back to Roger and sighed. "At the risk of sounding trite, we have got to stop meeting this way."

"I know." He pressed a kiss to her forehead. "Actually, that's why I came by."

Julie's gaze darted up and down the hallway before returning to him. "Oh yeah?"

"I have tomorrow night off."

"You do?" She squealed and clapped a hand over her mouth. "So do I!"

"I know." A slow, sexy grin slid across his face and he waggled his eyebrows.

"And?" Was he going to ask her out on a real date? Julie sent a silent prayer heavenward. Please, please, please…

He shrugged and started to turn away, a wicked gleam in his eyes. "I just thought I'd let you know."

Julie punched his arm. "What do I have to do? Beg?"

"For what?"

"You're impossible."

"Yeah, I am, aren't I?" He grinned.

Kim glanced around. "You two better figure it out quick, here she comes."

"How about it?" He grabbed her and pressed the hard ridge of his cock against her belly. "Tomorrow? A real date? I have reservations at the Red Lantern."

"Yes!" She flung her arms around his neck and kissed him full on the mouth and let him go just as quickly. "A real date, with food, and candles and se—" Kim nudged her in the back hard enough she stumbled into Roger.

"Nurse Lindeman," Kim said behind her. "Julie was just questioning Mr. Decker about the psych case he brought in."

Roger's lips twitched as if he forced back the smile threatening to take over his face.

The heat in Julie's cheeks deepened and she struggled with words. "Uh…yes…I was just questioning Mr. Decker about the…uh—"

"Psych case in Room 2. But now she's done, right, Julie? Mr. Marley is waiting in Room 2. Mustn't keep him waiting, must we. No ma'am." Kim hustled Julie past the head nurse and continued toward the room with the psych case.

Nurse Lindeman let them go, but as Julie passed her, she noted how her eyes narrowed and she nailed Roger with a piercing glare. "Aren't you the same cop that's been hanging around lately?"

"Come on." Kim tugged Julie down the hallway.

"But she'll chew him up and spit him out." Julie didn't feel right leaving Roger to handle Nurse Lindeman by himself.

"He's a big boy, he can manage all by himself. Besides, you have to fill me in on all the juicy details.

Julie's cheeks warmed as she recalled just how juicy the details had been. "No way."

"Hey, how am I supposed to live vicariously through you if you don't share?" Kim shoved her through the doorway.

"Get your own life!" With a last glance at Roger, Julie caught him winking at her over Nurse Lindeman's head. Tomorrow night was going to be great. She was finally going to have a real date, with real sex, and the best part was that she'd be with Roger.

"What's this about a psych case?" Nurse Lindeman was asking.

After Julie disappeared through a doorway, Roger dragged his gaze back to the woman in front of him.

"Ma'am?" What had she asked? He couldn't recall. Not after watching Julie's ass twitch all the way down the hall. So, he smiled his most charming smile, the one he reserved for the politicians' wives.

"If you'd get your mind off my nurse's ass for a moment, we could both do our jobs."

Her sharp words brought him back in focus. "Bob Marley, the guy I brought in a few minutes ago, was caught trying to stab some poor bum with a wooden stake."

"Huh? Why the hell did you bring him here? You should have taken him down to the station and booked him on assault charges."

Roger ignored the head nurse's attempt to tell him how to do his job. "I would have, except he sounded hysterical, a little deranged. I thought maybe you guys could test him for drugs or something. He was pretty upset, to the point of crazy. We had to strap him down. I left him with the doctor."

"Great. Just what we need. A nutcase stirring up trouble in my emergency room. Anything else you'd like to tell me?" Nurse Lindeman crossed her arms over her chest and her brows rose high on her forehead.

He knew what she wanted, but he avoided any mention of Julie. Although he'd like more time with her, he didn't want to get her fired from her job. "Yeah, Mr. Marley was screaming something about being a slayer and his job was to rid the world of vampires." Roger shrugged and grinned. "He's a live one."

"Thanks." Nurse Lindeman's lips twisted. "Remind me to return the favor some time."

"Don't mention it," he said lightly and turned to leave, but a hand caught his arm.

"By the way," she touched a finger to his chest. "Your buttons are mismatched and your fly is open." She turned away, a smile stretching across her face, a sparkle lighting her eyes.

Roger glanced down.

Busted.

For a moment he wished he could be swallowed by the floor, his face burned all the way out to the tips of his ears. Now he knew what was more embarrassing than getting caught in the act. Getting caught with your fly down by the head nurse.

Oh well, shit happens. He just hoped he didn't get Julie in too much trouble. Roger quickly adjusted the offending buttons and zipper. He couldn't get too bent, he had a date with Julie tomorrow night. A real, honest-to-God date. Not just a quick feel in the janitor's closet.

He rubbed his hands together and headed for his squad car and his waiting partner.

Chase leaned against the driver's door talking with a pretty little blonde in white scrubs and a blue lab coat. When he saw Roger, he straightened. "About time you showed up, partner." He gathered the blonde in his arms and kissed her like he was going to crawl down her throat or throw her on the hood of the squad car and bang her there. "I'll see you later, baby."

When he let her go, she staggered backward, her eyes glazed and a hand fluttering to her lips. "Call me?"

He winked. "You bet."

As he climbed into the passenger side of the squad car, Roger's lips twisted.

Chase eased behind the wheel and started the engine.

"You aren't going to call her, are you?" Roger's words were more of a statement than a question.

"Nope."

"Why do you do that?" He could imagine Julie's reaction if he kissed her like that and didn't call later. She'd be hurt, disappointed and then angry.

"Do what?"

"Kiss and run."

"You're one to be talking." Chase shot him a look, complete with raised eyebrows. "How long has your divorce been final?"

"Two years."

"And you've been out on how many dates?"

"None," he said. "But that's different. I haven't wanted to go out with another woman, until now."

"Buddy, you either qualify as a saint or deserve the dumbass-of-the-year award. I couldn't go two weeks without sex, much less two years." Chase slammed the car in drive and pulled out of the parking area into traffic.

Roger stared at the blur of streetlights skimming past his window. Two years. Two years since his marriage fell apart. Two years since he'd caught his wife sleeping with another cop. He hadn't trusted any woman since.

Until Julie. His fingers still tingled from the warmth and silkiness of her skin. He couldn't wait until tomorrow night. After a candlelit dinner at her favorite restaurant, they'd go back to his apartment for a little dessert. Sensuous music and soft lighting ought to set the mood for his planned seduction. He wanted to bury himself in

Julie and forget how much his ex-wife's deception had hurt.

Julie, the angel in nurse's clothing. Kind, gentle Julie with her strawberry blonde hair and pale, soft skin was just what he needed to get over Susan. His Julie would never lie to him like Susan had. She'd never lie to him or see another man on the side.

"So what did you decide? Are you a saint or a dumbass?" Chase's voice brought him back to the interior of the squad car.

"Neither."

"So when are you going to get into that nurse's pants? What's her name? Julia?"

"It's Julie and tomorrow. I mean, I asked her out tomorrow. But that doesn't mean I'm going to get into her pants." Although that's exactly where he'd been only moments before, in his mind.

"Then you're definitely a dumbass."

The radios on their shoulders squawked. "All units in the vicinity of Main and Lamar Streets, assault in progress. Please respond."

"That's us." Roger pressed the talk button on his radio to inform the dispatcher they'd take the call and their estimated time of arrival. Then he settled back in his seat, glad the diversion had taken Chase's mind off the subject of Julie and her pants.

When the squad car stopped in the location given, Roger didn't see anyone at first. "Do you think it was a crank call?"

"I think I saw movement in that alley. Let's go." Chase shoved the car in park and leapt out, drawing the Glock from his holster.

Before Chase could round the car, Roger took off at a dead run toward the alley, hugging the buildings along the sidewalk. Adrenaline packed his veins, shooting blood to his brain, clearing his hearing, vision and thinking processes to hone in on his quarry. This was the reason he loved his job. Not the nights of boring patrols, hauling in drunks or cleaning up prostitutes.

No, he loved going after the bad guys and bringing them down. Face it. He was a thrill junkie. The night shift was the best place to find them.

When he reached the alley, he stood with his back to the wall and waited for Chase to catch up. With a nod toward his partner, he stepped into the dark passage. A shadow moved beside a dumpster. It appeared to be a man. A man carrying another person. A woman.

"Halt! Or I'll shoot!"

A wicked rumble erupted from the shadows and built into the sound of laughter, a deep masculine laugh. The shadow straightened, the laughter stopped and piercing red eyes turned toward Roger. "Toy cops."

"Let her go." Roger called out.

"By all means." The stranger dropped the body he

was holding. It fell to the pavement with a dull *whomp.* "Now what? Gonna arrest me?"

"Step to the side and lay face to the ground."

"No, I don't think so. I don't like to play by the rules."

Before Roger could react, the man leapt the six yards between them in one bound.

His finger squeezed on the trigger and his Glock erupted into the man's belly.

The man only laughed, seized Roger's weapon and slung it to the side.

Chase unloaded six rounds in rapid succession into the man's chest.

Other than jerking at the impact, the bullets did nothing but make holes through his body.

He lifted Roger by the front of his uniform and slung him ten feet across the pavement. He landed in the street on his back, all the wind knocked from his lungs, his head pounding hard against the asphalt.

Chase landed beside him.

The stranger stared down at them, his white-blond hair standing up straight in ragged spikes. A smile crept across his face. "I just stopped for a snack. Thanks for the entertainment." Then the man was gone so fast Roger had to blink to make sure his vision wasn't impaired by the fall.

Recovering first, Roger sucked air into his lungs in a desperate gasp. "Fuck! What was that?"

When Chase didn't answer right away, Roger rolled over to check him out. "You all right, buddy?"

His partner pressed a hand to his head. "Did you get the number of that truck that hit me?"

"No shit. I unloaded on him and the bullets didn't even faze him." Roger stared into the darkness.

"That was one scary son of a bitch."

"Yeah. I'm beginning to rethink my career choice."

THANK GOD FOR 3:00 A.M. Julie slipped into her sweater, grabbed her purse and headed for the exit. On her way out, she passed by her dark-haired friend leading a patient into an exam room. "See ya the day after tomorrow, Kim."

"Don't do anything I wouldn't do on your really hot date the Cop Candy."

Julie paused, and rested her hands on her hips. "Is there anything you wouldn't do?"

With a frown and a glance at the ceiling, Kim answered, "Nope. Nothing I can think of. So that leaves it wide open. Use your imagination."

Julie turned to leave, a smile on her face.

"Hey," Kim called after her.

"More advice?" Julie fisted a hand on one hip.

"If you need to borrow my Kama Sutra book, just stop by tomorrow anytime."

The old lady leaning on Kim nodded. "That Kama

Sutra book saved my marriage, it did. Although some of those positions are physically impossible at my age."

Julie ducked out the side door to the sound of Kim's giggles.

Out in the parking garage, Julie climbed into her car and turned the key.

Click.

She tried again.

Click.

She checked the battery gauge. "Ah, shit."

Her battery was deader than dead.

"Fuck!"

Although she only lived four blocks from the hospital, the thought of walking home on her aching feet brought tears to her eyes. The hospital parking lot was completely empty of people. She could wait another two hours until Kim got off, or call a cab. Hell, she could walk her butt home faster than it would take a cab to get there.

As she climbed out of her car, and slung her purse over her shoulder, every bone and muscle in her body sagged.

Damn cars. Why couldn't they break down at a more opportune time, like on the way to work when her feet didn't hurt?

She strode down the garage ramp and out onto the sidewalk, working up anger as she walked. No, mechanical problems had to wait until frickin' three o'clock in the morning when not a single car passed by. When only the drunks and bums wandered around. She sure as hell hoped they wouldn't bother her on her way home. Thank goodness there was no such thing as the monsters that Bob Marley had ranted about earlier. She owed Roger for that one. The man was delusional. All his talk about vampires and demons.

Good thing Julie didn't believe in all that nonsense.

Because if she did, she'd be a little afraid tonight. She glanced up at the full moon ringed in an eerie red glow. Yup. A more superstitious woman would be running back to the hospital and waiting for Kim to get off to bum a ride home. But not Julie. She was the levelheaded one. Not easily spooked. "No, sir. I don't believe in all that Goth vampire shit."

Just as she spoke the words out loud, a man appeared in front of her. A very tall, broad-shouldered man with blond, spiked hair and dark eyes. No. Make that red eyes. He reminded her of a bulkier Spike from a Buffy rerun.

"Maybe you should believe," he said, his voice more a growl than anything else.

Julie dropped back a step, swallowed a scream and said the first thing that came to her mind. "Geesh! You shouldn't jump out at people in the middle of the night. I could have died of a heart attack."

"I doubt you'll die of a heart attack tonight."

"Only because I'm in pretty good shape and eat healthy." She stared hard at him, though her pulse beat at an erratic rate. This man, with all his bulging muscles, could

easily take her, rape her or anything else he had a mind to. She was a lone woman armed only with her purse.

Her hand shifted to the bag. She did have a small canister of mace at the bottom of her oversized bag, if she could get to it before he killed her.

"If you want money, you can have whatever is in my wallet. I'll get it." Like he couldn't see right through her ruse? She jammed her hand inside her handbag and rummaged frantically.

He plucked the purse from her shoulder and tossed it and the mace several yards away.

"Okaaayyy. I guess I'll just have to use my black belt in karate." She dropped into a crouch, her hands in chop position and yelled like she'd seen the bad guys do in the Jackie Chan flicks. Not that she knew any more than that. But maybe she could bluff her way out of a potentially lose-lose situation.

Where the hell was a cop when you needed one? Where was Roger? He should still be on duty. Why couldn't he drive by about now and rescue her? "So? What's it gonna be? Are you going to let me by without a hassle, or am I going to have to take you down?" *Please let me by. Please.*

ABOUT THE AUTHOR

Twenty years of livin' and lovin' on a South Texas ranch raising horses, cattle, goats, ostriches and emus left an indelible impression on Myla Jackson, one she likes to instill in her red-hot stories. Myla pens wildly sexy, fun adventures of all genres including historical westerns, medieval tales, romantic suspense, contemporary romance and paranormal beasties of all shapes and sexy sizes. She lives in the tree-covered hills of Northwest Arkansas with her husband of more than 20 years and her muses—the human-wanna-be canines—Chewy and Sweetpea.

To learn more about Myla Jackson and her alter ego Elle James visit:

www.mylajackson.com
mylajackson@mylajackson.com

Ugly Stick Saloon Series

Boots & Chaps (#1)

Boots & Sex Ed (#2)

Boots & Leather (#3)

Boots & Promises (#4)

Boots & Bareback (#5)

Boots & Dirty Tricks (#6)

Boots & Lace (#7)

Boots & Roses (#8)

Boots & Buckles (#9)

Boots & the Wishes (#10)

Boots & Twisters (#11)

Boots & the Bachelor (#12)

Boots & The Rogue (#13)

Boots & The Heartbreaker (#14)

Boots & Wings (#15)

Tomb Raider Trouble

Trouble with Harry

Trouble with Will

Trouble with Mitch